PISTOL PERSUASION

When Fury came awake, it was instantly, with every nerve alert for danger.

"I'll scream," said Laurel Whitelaw.

"You do and I'll kill Fury and your two brothers." The second voice belonged to Lester Oakley. His big hands were clamped on Laurel's shoulders, trying to pull her closer to him.

"Leave my sister alone, you bastard!" shouted Pate as he tackled Oakley. He looped wild punches at Oakley's head, but the older man blocked them and drove up a blow of his own. Oakley's face contorted with hate and anger, and he lifted his foot, ready to drive the heel of his boot down into Pate's face.

Fury's gun whispered out of its holster and the sound of the hammer being drawn back was clearly audible. "That's enough," he said, his voice as cold as the air around them. . . .

* * *

SPECIAL PREVIEW!

Turn to the back of this book
for a special excerpt
from an exciting new Western . . .

GUNPOINT

. . . The shattering story
of a deadly blood feud by America's new star
of the classic Western, Giles Tippette.

DON'T MISS THESE
AUTHENTIC WESTERN SERIES
FROM THE BERKLEY PUBLISHING GROUP

FURY by Jim Austin
Meet John Fury. Gunfighter. Legend. Where there's trouble, there's Fury.

THE HORSEMEN by Gary McCarthy
The epic story of a frontier family's glorious dream, raising horses in the untamed West.

NORTHWEST DESTINY by Bill Gulick
The award-winning author's acclaimed trilogy of white men and Indians bound by blood.

SONS OF TEXAS by Tom Early
"A series that brings to mind L'Amour's Sackett family saga." —*Booklist*

SHILOH by Dalton Walker
The classic adventures of a Civil War veteran turned bounty hunter.

LONG RIDER by Clay Dawson
A white man raised by Indians. Long Rider was caught between the blood and hate of two peoples.

CREED by Bryce Harte
Based on actual records, this epic series captures life in a Texas town shattered by the Civil War.

BROTHERS IN BLOOD by Daniel St. James
On the Canadian border, a U.S. Marshal and a Canadian Mountie are bound by a loyalty only brothers can share.

Westerns by Giles Tippette
The new star of the classic western novel, Tippette captures the American dream in the saga of the Williams clan.

FURY

BLOOD RANSOM

JIM AUSTIN

BERKLEY BOOKS, NEW YORK

BLOOD RANSOM

A Berkley Book / published by arrangement with
the author

PRINTING HISTORY
Berkley edition / October 1992

ISBN: 0-425-13485-7

A BERKLEY BOOK ® TM 757,375
Berkley Books are published by The Berkley Publishing Group,
200 Madison Avenue, New York, New York 10016.
The name "BERKLEY" and the "B" logo
are trademarks belonging to Berkley Publishing Corporation.

PRINTED IN THE UNITED STATES OF AMERICA

10 9 8 7 6 5 4 3 2 1

For
Tom and Ginger Johnson

FURY

BLOOD RANSOM

CHAPTER
1

· · · · · · · · · · · · · · · · · · · ·

Six-Shooter Junction. That was what the stagecoach drivers called the settlement of Waco, Texas, when they warned their passengers not to wander off while the teams were being changed at the stopover there. Anybody who did was liable to catch a bullet for their trouble.

In the few years since the town had been laid out by a land agent named Jacob de Cordova in 1849, Waco had grown quickly. Captain Shapley Ross, a former Texas Ranger who had been stationed at nearby Fort Fisher, had opened a ferry across the Brazos River near the springs that had drawn the area's first settlers, the Waco Indians. Traffic on the ferry was brisk as folks headed across the Brazos toward west Texas. The rich black soil along the river was perfect both for farming and for growing grass for cattle to graze on. Farms and ranches sprang up along both sides of the Brazos. There was still some Indian trouble from time to time, sure, but you could stand on the bank of the river and look around at the growing community and sense that civilization had come to this part of central Texas.

And with civilization had come the outlaws—card sharps, soiled doves, petty cheats, and men running from crimes in their past straight toward crimes in their future. Saloons, whorehouses, and gambling dens rose alongside churches, schools, and the so-called respectable businesses. If Waco followed the pattern of other frontier towns, eventually the upstanding citizens would band together and force most of the lawless element to head farther west. That day was still in the future.

John Fury rode into Waco late in the afternoon of an April day after crossing the Brazos on Captain Ross's ferry. He was tired, having come all the way from the Red River in the last two-and-a-half days, across sparsely settled country that didn't

1

offer a man much chance to relax. The northern third of Texas was still Indian country, and Fury had slept with one eye open the last couple of nights.

He rode a rangy lineback dun that wasn't much for looks but could run all day when it had to. A pack mule trailed behind him at the end of a plaited rawhide rope. The mule got stubborn every so often, as mules do, and Fury had spent part of the day pulling on the reata and trying to get the damned beast to move. He was starting to think there was some truth to that old saying about having to hit a mule in the head with a gun butt just to get his attention.

Fury reined up in front of a saloon called Fogle's Place, according to the crudely painted sign over the door. He swung down from the saddle, a broad-shouldered six-footer with the natural grace of a man accustomed to trouble. His broad-brimmed, flat-crowned black hat had turned grayish from trail dust. Before he went into the saloon, he took the hat off and hit it against a thigh clad in fringed buckskin pants tucked into high-topped black boots. As he did that, he ran the fingers of his other hand through a thatch of brown hair that was touched in places with gray.

A gunbelt was strapped around his lean waist. In the holster on his right hip rode a Colt's Third Model Dragoon pistol. A Bowie knife was on his left hip, and tucked into a saddleboot on the dun was a Sharps carbine. Fury was well armed, but no more so than many men who rode the frontier. He wouldn't have called the guns the tools of his trade—but that wasn't far from the truth.

He put his hat on again, tied the dun and the mule to the hitch rack in front of the saloon, and stepped up onto Fogle's low porch. He would get a drink in here to cut the trail dust, maybe some food if the place had a cook, then look for a place to bed down.

The sun was still up, so he could have pushed on. But he was more interested in finding an inside bed for a change. During the past few months he had spent nearly every night on the trail.

Fogle's was a small place with a narrow barroom, with the bar running down the left-hand wall. Tables filled the floor space. At one of the tables in the rear, a poker game was going on, but a glance at the coins and bills piled in the center of the table told Fury the stakes were low. The players looked to be cowhands and farmers, with not a professional gambler in the bunch. Fury decided to pass on the game, even though there were some empty chairs at the table. It probably wouldn't be enough of a challenge to interest him.

There were four other customers leaning on the bar. Fury joined them and said to a bartender wearing a collarless white shirt, "Beer, as cool as you can get it."

"We keep the kegs down in the cellar," the bartender told him. "Keeps 'em nice and cool, mister." He drew the beer, slid it across the hardwood to Fury, and scooped up the coin Fury dropped on the bar.

Just as promised, the beer was cool, and Fury took a long, grateful swallow of it. Then he turned halfway around, leaned an elbow on the bar, and surveyed the rest of the room. Only about a fourth of the tables were occupied. It wasn't late enough in the day for the saloon's business to start picking up.

There was only one woman in the place, and she was sitting at one of the tables with a couple of cowboys. Her brown hair was done up in an elaborate arrangement of curls on top of her head, and a pair of bright yellow feathers were stuck in it. The feathers matched the tight-bodiced dress she was wearing. Fury put her age around thirty—no newcomer to the game, but not yet worn out by it either.

"If you're looking at Maddie, mister, I wouldn't get any ideas. Those boys she's with wouldn't take kindly to anybody else butting in."

The low-voiced warning came from the bartender. Fury gave him a faint smile, said, "I'm not looking for trouble."

That was true; he wasn't. But he didn't believe in backing down from it if it came his way.

For the moment, though, he was more interested in food than he was in a woman, even a good-looking one like Maddie. He went on to the bartender, "You got a hash-slinger in this place?"

"The saloon, you mean?"

Fury nodded.

" 'Fraid not. Closest eating place is Ezra's, a couple doors down."

"Any good?"

The bartender shrugged. "Not bad. Don't know that I'd go so far as to call it *good*."

"That'll do, I reckon." Fury drained the rest of his beer, slid the empty mug across the bar, and turned to leave. As he strode toward the batwings, he sensed someone watching him. He didn't look back, though, until he had reached the doorway.

Then a glance over his shoulder told him the watching eyes belonged to the woman called Maddie. Fury smiled at her and went out, thinking that he might have to pay a return visit to Fogle's after he'd eaten.

As it turned out, the food at Ezra's was pretty good. The standard fare was roast beef and potatoes, but Ezra's wife was a stout little Mexican woman who liked to throw in some beans and peppers and tortillas, too. Fury put away a good-sized plate of the stuff, washed down with strong, black coffee. A few more drinks, a good night's sleep, and he'd feel damned near human again, he thought as he strolled back toward Fogle's.

The place was busier now, and the stakes in the poker game had gotten higher. Fury again decided against sitting in.

Maddie was there, sitting at the same table with the same punchers. The men looked like they had downed quite a few drinks since Fury was in there before. Both of them were red-faced, and their laughter as they talked with Maddie was loud and raucous. Nobody paid any real attention to them, but Fury noticed the other patrons of the saloon seemed to give their table a wide berth. Maybe the two of them had reputations as troublemakers.

Trouble was the last thing he wanted tonight. He skirted the table and headed for the bar. Only problem was that Maddie had her eyes on him again as he went by.

"Hey, Maddie," Fury heard one of the men say, "what you lookin' at that damn drifter for? You're with us, 'member?"

"Sure, Billy," she told him. "I'm with you."

But Fury knew without looking that her eyes had cut back over to him even as she said it.

He grimaced as he put his hands flat on the bar and waited for the bartender to come over. Warning bells were going off in his head. He'd ridden the frontier for a long time, been in a lot of fights. Sometimes you couldn't see them coming, but sometimes you could. This was one of those times.

What he ought to do was turn around, walk out of here, and find a livery stable for the animals and a hotel for himself. The sun was going down, and he was tired enough to go to bed with the chickens for a change. But he wanted to top off that meal with another beer or two, and he was just stubborn enough to stay here until he had done that.

He signaled to the bartender, and the man finally ambled over. The bartender drew the beer, took Fury's money, and turned away to drop the coin in the cash box. Fury lifted the beer.

He only had it halfway to his mouth when a soft footstep sounded right behind him. Pausing, he glanced over his shoulder and saw what he hoped he wouldn't. Maddie stood there, and although she spoke to the bartender, her eyes were fastened squarely on Fury as she said, "We need another bottle, Ted."

The bartender frowned. "Haven't Billy and Judd had about enough? They've been in here since right after lunch."

"I can't make up their minds for them. And they say they want another bottle."

"They keep drinking like that, they ain't going to be much use to you later," the bartender said with a snort of disgust.

"I know." Maddie's lips curved in a smile as she looked at Fury and went on, "I guess I'll have to find somebody else to show me a good time."

She wanted him to say something; that much was obvious. So he commented, "That shouldn't be too hard, ma'am, not for somebody as pretty as you."

Her smile widened. "Why, thank you, Mister . . . ?"

"Fury, John Fury."

He could tell she'd never heard of him, and he was grateful for that. A reputation came in handy sometimes, but most of the time it was a damned bother.

"Hey, Maddie!" called one of the cowboys at the table. "You gettin' us that bottle or not?"

"Coming right up, Judd," she told him. Turning her gaze back to Fury, she said, "Maybe you'd like to join us?"

Fury had to grin at the sudden look of concern on the bartender's face. The man didn't want his place busted up by a fight. "I don't think that would be a very good idea," Fury said quietly. "Your friends are getting a little impatient."

"Let 'em," Maddie snapped.

"Some other time," said Fury, making his voice gentle to take any sting out of the refusal.

"You're turning me down?" Maddie sounded like she couldn't believe it.

"Like I said, some other time."

Her brown eyes narrowed and began to glitter with anger. Fury realized she had been hoping to provoke a fight. Some women seemed to enjoy that, seeing men battling over them. Fury had never really understood the appeal of it. He picked up his beer and drank.

The bartender held out a bottle of whiskey, extending his arm across the bar to the woman. "Take the bottle and go on back to them before they get any antsier," he told Maddie.

"Sure," she said sullenly, snatching the rotgut from him and stalking back to the table.

"Sorry about that, mister," the bartender said to Fury. "I can see you don't want any kind of ruckus—"

A sharp, loud voice from the table where Maddie and the two cowboys sat cut off the bartender's statement. One of the men had scraped his chair back and exclaimed, "He said *what?*"

Fury set his beer down, closed his eyes for a second, sighed, and said, "Oh, hell."

He turned around and saw that both the cowboys were on their feet now, the red glare of the setting sun spilling through the grimy front windows of the saloon behind them. The babble of conversation in the room died away as the customers realized something was about to happen. The two punchers glowered at Fury as Maddie leaned forward in her chair and said urgently, "Don't worry about it, boys. I don't care what that drifter called me!"

The sly smile on her face as she glanced at Fury put the lie to her words.

"Whore or no whore, you're still a lady, and nobody's goin' to insult you!" said one of the cowboys. He pointed a finger at Fury. "You take it back and tell the lady you're sorry, mister!"

"Nothing to take back," Fury said calmly. "I didn't insult her."

"Now you're callin' her a liar!" exclaimed the other cowboy.

"Now, Billy, Judd, just take it easy," warned the bartender. "I don't want any trouble in here."

"Shut up, Fogle," growled the one called Billy. He clenched his fists and stepped forward. "Reckon Judd and me are goin' to have to teach this jasper a little lesson in manners."

"You bound and determined to go through with this, boys?" Fury asked.

Their glares and ready stances were all the answer Fury needed.

He sighed again. "Why don't we take it outside, then? No need to cause a lot of breakage in here."

"To hell with that—and to hell with you, mister!"

Billy scooped up a ladderback chair and flung it straight at Fury's head.

CHAPTER
2

....

On that same evening in April, a buggy rolled along the road that followed the Brazos west out of Waco. Calling it a road might be stretching things a little, but it was more than the game trail it had once been. A young man named Joshua Whitelaw was at the reins, guiding the big draft horse that was pulling the buggy. Beside Joshua on the seat was his sister, Felicia, an attractive young woman with long, blonde hair drawn up into a neat bun on her head. The rear of the buggy was filled with packages from the shopping trip that had taken Joshua and Felicia into Waco that afternoon.

"Isn't it a lovely evening, Joshua?"

He nodded in reply to his sister's question. "Only a fool would say no."

By morning, the air might be cool, but now, as the red orb of the sun dipped below the western horizon, the warmth of the afternoon lingered. The grass on the rolling hills along the river was beginning to green, and bright bursts of color were visible among the green. Bluebonnets, daisies, Indian paintbrush, all kinds of wildflowers were starting to bloom, and each day brought more of them. The oaks that dotted the hills were putting out leaves, too.

The Whitelaw family had lived in Waco for over a year, and both Joshua and Felicia knew how beautiful the place could be in the spring. A few miles farther up this road sat the house Preston Whitelaw had built when he brought his wife and children to Texas from Alabama. It was a large, whitewashed frame structure that bore a resemblance to the plantation the Whitelaws had left behind them. But this was a ranchhouse. Preston ran several hundred head of cattle on his spread, as well as a sizable horse herd. It was a successful operation, and the house was one of the showplaces along the river.

8

Unlike some of the other plantation owners who had moved west, Whitelaw kept no slaves. He paid a few ranch hands honest wages, but primarily he believed in the value of hard work for himself, his oldest son Joshua, and the two younger boys, Peyton and Frank. His wife Muriel and the two girls, Felicia and Laurel, cared for the vegetable garden, did the cooking and cleaning, and made many of the clothes the family wore.

Not that Whitelaw was some sort of miser. The house was furnished comfortably, almost luxuriously, and all the members of the family had store-bought clothes for special occasions, such as this trip into town today by Joshua and Felicia. Joshua wore a dark suit and a broad-brimmed brown hat, and his sister had on a pretty blue dress and a matching bonnet.

Preston Whitelaw believed in fine horses, too. The animal pulling the buggy was a prime specimen of what people were already calling the finest bunch of horseflesh in this part of the state. Joshua had the horse moving along at a steady clip, and the swaying of the buggy had a rhythm to it that could almost rock a man to sleep. Joshua lifted a hand to his mouth as he yawned.

The sudden whoops and gunshots jerked him back fully awake.

Joshua twisted his head around, staring in horror at a grove of oak trees to the south. A dozen Indians came boiling out of those trees, shouting and firing their rifles in the air. Felicia screamed at the sight of them.

This was no time to let fear overwhelm him, Joshua knew. Their only hope lay in quick action. He flapped the reins against the back of the horse and let out a yell. A short whip was socketed in a holder near his left hand. He snatched it out and laid the lash on the horse with another shout. The animal jumped, surprised by this treatment from the normally gentle Joshua, but it surged forward into a gallop, pulling the buggy along behind it.

"Hang on!" cried Joshua. Next to him, Felicia took a firm grip on the seat of the buggy to keep from being thrown out as the vehicle bounced over the ruts of the trail.

Joshua glanced to his left. The Indians were still coming on, angling now in an effort to intercept the racing buggy. In the gloom of evening, Joshua couldn't make out their features, but he could see their bare chests streaked with war paint and the feathers that decorated the long, dark hair of the men. They rode swift ponies and carried rifles, the weapons no doubt stolen from white men they had slaughtered.

Pushing his coat back, Joshua reached underneath it and found the .36-caliber Colt Navy revolver holstered at his waist. He drew the gun, aimed across his body at the Indians, cocked, and fired. The blast made Felicia scream again.

It was difficult controlling the horse with only one hand for the reins, but Joshua knew he had to discourage the savages. He cocked the pistol again and fired it, but just as before, he couldn't tell that the shot had any effect on the Indians. They were still coming on, riding hard toward the river. Joshua thought fleetingly about leaving the trail, but with the Brazos so close on his right hand and the Indians galloping in from the left, there was just no place to go.

Except back, maybe.

Joshua hauled hard on the reins even as that desperate thought crossed his mind. The Indians were trying to get in front of the buggy to head them off, so if he could turn the vehicle around and head back toward Waco, there was a chance they could outrun the Indians to the edge of town. A slim chance, to be sure, but better than plunging ahead into certain death.

And he was sure that was what it would mean for him if the Indians caught them. They might spare Felicia's life, but she would wish they had killed her before they were through with her.

In the fading light, he couldn't see the Indians well enough to tell which tribe they were from. Most of the time, the Wacos and the Cherokees around the settlement didn't cause any trouble. The Comanches who came raiding from the west were a much bigger threat. These Indians who were chasing them were probably Comanche, Joshua thought as he holstered his pistol and pulled the horse into a tight turn.

The buggy was jolted hard as its wheels left the trail momentarily and rolled over a stretch of rugged ground. Joshua and Felicia were both bounced up off the hard seat for an instant. Then the buggy was back on the beaten path, and it began to pick up speed again as Joshua lashed at the horse and shouted encouragement to it.

Waco was too far away for its lights to be visible in the gathering darkness. Joshua poured it on, urging the horse to greater and greater speed. Even over the pounding of hooves and the squealing of wheels, however, Joshua could hear the war whoops of the Indians drawing nearer behind them.

Maybe someone had heard the shooting and would come to their assistance, he thought. It was possible. There were quite a few settlers living along the river, and folks in these parts were quick to turn out to help a neighbor in trouble.

If this didn't qualify, Joshua didn't know what would.

This particular stretch of the Brazos was more sparsely settled than others, though. The nearest homestead was about a mile back, Joshua remembered. It was almost like the Indians had chosen this spot to attack knowing it was unlikely that anybody would help their victims.

Felicia twisted around on the seat and raised herself slightly to peer through the gap between the buggy's canopy and the rear wall of canvas. "They're getting closer, Joshua!" she cried. "Give me your gun!"

Joshua didn't hesitate. All the Whitelaw youngsters, including the girls, had been taught to use guns by their father. He slid the Colt out of its holster and pressed the walnut butt into Felicia's outstretched hand.

Balancing herself precariously on the seat, Felicia used both hands to grip the gun and lift it to the gap. She poked the muzzle through the opening, eared back the hammer with her thumbs, and pressed the trigger. The revolver blasted deafeningly again, and the recoil almost knocked her off the seat.

That was the third shot from the gun, and Felicia knew there were only two more in the cylinder. Joshua always kept the hammer resting on an empty. For one wild moment, she thought she should save those two shots for Joshua and herself in case the Indians caught them. Better a slug through the brain than slow death by torture.

Then her jaw firmed in anger. Preston and Muriel Whitelaw had not raised any of their children to give up. Felicia pulled back the Colt's hammer, aimed as best she could through the dust being kicked up by the buggy's careening passage, and squeezed the trigger again.

Once again the kick of the gun as it exploded nearly knocked her off the seat. But she caught herself, squinted behind them, and let out a shout as she saw that one of the Indian ponies was riderless now. "Got one!"

Joshua felt a surge of exultation. They weren't going to die before inflicting some damage of their own, at least. He tried to coax more speed out of the horse, but it was a lost cause. The animal was already giving it everything he had.

And the Indians were only a few yards behind now.

One of the war-painted riders urged his mount up even closer. The pony came abreast of the buggy, and the Indian aimed one-handed with the rifle he carried. He was on Joshua's side of the buggy, and as the young man spotted the threat out of the corner of his eye, he cried, "Felicia! Over here!"

He leaned forward, and Felicia fired over the top of his head. The bullet hit the Indian and made him sag forward, throwing his horse off stride. The animal lost its balance and went down, its front legs buckling. The Indian screamed as he was thrown over the horse's head. The horse rolled over him, abruptly cutting off that scream. Shaken but unhurt, the horse got to its feet and raced off, leaving behind it a gory mess that had been its former owner.

That was the last shot in the Colt, though. There would be no chance to reload, not in this bouncing, swaying buggy that was taking all of Joshua's concentration to control. More Indians swept up around them.

"Get down, Felicia!" shouted Joshua, taking one hand from the reins long enough to push his sister toward the floorboard of the vehicle.

A couple of the raiders cut loose again just as Joshua shoved Felicia down. The rifle bullets slammed into him, making him slew sideways on the seat. The reins slipped from his fingers and slithered forward, dropping to the ground behind the horse.

Felicia felt something warm and wet on her face and looked up to see Joshua lying on the seat, blood welling from his mouth and dripping on her. The front of his shirt was covered with blood as well. She shrieked and writhed away from him. He was still alive, she could tell that, but life was fading fast from his eyes. Even as she watched in horror, his eyes glazed over in death.

The Indians were closing in around the buggy now. One of them rode up beside the horse and leaned over to grab its harness, pulling it to a stop. The others sent up a round of triumphant whoops as they surrounded the vehicle.

Felicia forced herself to move, rolling out of the buggy and trying to dart between two of the ponies as her feet hit the ground. She couldn't outrun the Indians on foot, of course, but her pioneer spirit wouldn't allow her to just wait passively for whatever fate had in store for her.

One of the Indians knocked her bonnet off and tangled his dirty fingers in her long, blonde hair, jerking her to a painful stop. She cried out as she was thrown to the ground. A few feet away, another savage sprang into the buggy, grasped Joshua's blood-stained coat, and slung the young man's body out. Several more Indians fired their rifles into the corpse, making it jump from the impact of the bullets in a ghastly semblance of life.

Felicia was hauled to her feet again. One of the men grasped her arms from behind while others stroked her hair and fondled her breasts. She struggled wildly, but her strength was no match for theirs.

Suddenly, the brutal game was interrupted. Gunshots rang out in the distance. Two men appeared at the top of a nearby hill, riding hell-for-leather toward the Brazos and firing six-shooters as they came. One of the Indians snapped out a guttural command, and most of the savages who had dismounted sprang back onto their ponies.

The one holding Felicia began to drag her with him toward his horse. She screamed again and tried frantically to twist away from him. Even though Joshua was dead, if she could get loose now, there was a chance she would survive. The Indians clearly didn't have any stomach for facing two well-armed, angry men.

Terror gave Felicia added strength. She managed to pull away from her captor for a second, but before she could take more than a step, he fell on her again, and this time he drove a fist against the side of her head, stunning her. She felt him half-carrying, half-dragging her over to his mount, felt him pick her up and sling her over the animal's back. There was nothing she could do to stop him.

The two would-be rescuers weren't close enough. They were on the outer edge of pistol range, and their shots failed to down any of the Indians. Shouting out their defiance, the raiders galloped away from the stalled buggy and the body of Joshua Whitelaw sprawled beside it. A few more wild shots followed them but did no harm.

Felicia was in a daze now, only vaguely aware of what was happening. She knew the Indians were carrying her off. But the men who had tried to stop them would find the buggy and Joshua's body, and they would carry the news of Felicia's kidnapping back to Waco.

Her father wouldn't let the Indians keep her. She was sure of that. If she could stay alive long enough, Preston Whitelaw would find a way somehow to get his daughter back.

If she could just stay alive . . .

CHAPTER
3

....

Fury ducked instinctively, letting the chair Billy had thrown sail over his head. There was a crash behind him as it landed, and Fogle let out a yelp. The bartender had either been hit by the chair or was just dismayed at the damage it had caused. Either way, Fury didn't have time to give much of a damn. Billy and Judd were both charging at him, fists clenched.

Judd was closer and was going to get there first. Fury pivoted toward him and flung up his left arm to block Judd's first punch. Fury threw one of his own, a hard, straight right that caught Judd flush on the nose and rocked him back, blood spurting from pulped nostrils. He howled in pain.

That gave Billy the opportunity to land a punch, however. The blow caught Fury on the side of the head and knocked him back against the bar. The edge of the hardwood dug painfully into his kidneys. Fury gritted his teeth, ducked under Billy's next punch, and slammed a left and a right into the young cowboy's belly.

The temptation was strong in him to palm out his Dragoon and shoot the two sons of bitches. It wasn't their fault they were stupid enough to let Maddie goad them into this senseless fight. Well, maybe it was, but being stupid didn't mean they deserved to die. Fury crashed another punch into Billy's jaw. He'd settle this with fists if he could, he decided.

Judd had recovered his balance and now leaped back into the fracas, the lower half of his beard-stubbled face covered with blood from his broken nose. He lunged at Fury, arms widespread. Fury tried to dart out of the way, but there wasn't room. Judd's arms went around him and tightened in a bear hug. The man lowered his head and butted Fury in the jaw.

Fighting off a red haze of pain and dizziness, Fury managed to swing around, taking Judd with him. Judd's arms were clamped so tightly around him that he couldn't breathe, and he was begin-

15

ning to get lightheaded. Over the pounding of the blood in his ears, he heard shouts coming from the spectators in the saloon. Maddie's shrill cries came through particularly well.

Fury set his feet and drove forward, catching Judd between him and the bar. Judd's back arched over the hardwood. He gasped from the impact and loosened his grip on Fury.

Fury worked an arm free and brought the heel of his hand up against Judd's chin, driving his head even farther back. Judd had to let go or Fury would have broken his neck.

There was a swishing sound behind Fury. He leaped aside just as Billy brought an empty whiskey bottle down where Fury's head had been an instant earlier. Thrown off balance by the miss, Billy stumbled forward and collided with Judd.

Fury drove an elbow into Billy's back, keeping him pinned against Judd and the bar. He grabbed the back of Billy's head, tangling his fingers in the cowpoke's long hair, and shoved it sharply forward. Billy's forehead banged against Judd's with a dull thud.

Both men went limp and slid to the sawdust-sprinkled floor.

Fury dragged air into his lungs and became aware that silence had fallen in the saloon. He looked around and saw the other patrons staring at him. He had already guessed that Billy and Judd had reputations as troublemakers, and these folks had probably never expected one man to be able to stand up to them. Not only stand up to them, but defeat them.

Maddie looked more shocked than anybody else.

Fogle came out from behind the bar, stared down at the limp bodies of the two young men, and shook his head. "I figured I'd take the money from your pockets to pay for the damage after they'd had their fun," he said to Fury. "Didn't think they'd be the ones who wound up on the floor."

Fury glanced behind the bar and saw the scattering of broken glass and the puddle of spilled whiskey from the bottles that had been on shelves on the wall. The chair that had shattered the bottles was broken as well. "I reckon you can take the money out of their pockets," grunted Fury as he jerked a thumb at Billy and Judd.

Fogle just shook his head again. "They'd hold it against me. I know those boys. They'd come back later and really bust up the place."

"Oh, hell." Fury bent over the senseless men and delved in their pockets, coming up with a few wadded bills and some change. He plunked it down on the bar and said, "That ought to cover it. Just tell them I did it, not you. If they've got any complaints, they can look me up. I'll be around for a day or two."

The bartender hesitated, then nodded nervously and swept the bills and coins off the hardwood and into his palm. Clutching the money tightly, he said, "Thanks, mister."

Fury picked up his hat, knocked the sawdust off it, and settled it on his head. "I'll finish that beer now."

No sooner had he picked up the glass than Maddie was at his side again. "That was really something," she said breathlessly.

He saw the way her eyes shone, the way her breasts rose and fell quickly. The fight had aroused her. Now that Billy and Judd were out of the picture, he knew he would have no trouble taking her back to whatever crib she used. Nobody else in here would interfere, not after what they had seen.

The only trouble was, Fury couldn't help but remember how Maddie had orchestrated the whole thing. Billy and Judd had thrown the punches, but she had pulled their strings.

"Not interested," he said curtly. "And before you get your back up and try to sic somebody else on me, you'd better know—I'll kill the next man who braces me in this town."

His voice was low enough so that it carried only to Maddie and to Fogle, who had retreated behind the bar. The cold words made both of them go pale.

"No call to feel that way, mister . . ." ventured Fogle. Maddie didn't say anything, but she at least had the decency to look a little abashed. Fury just lifted the beer to his mouth again.

This time he actually got to drink some of it before the street outside erupted with hoofbeats and gunshots.

The commotion drew the attention of the saloon's patrons. They flocked to the windows and the batwinged door to watch two men ride past at breakneck speed, firing their pistols in the air and shouting, "Indians! Indians!"

An uneasy stir went through the crowd in the barroom. It was unlikely that Indians would attack a settlement as big as Waco, but something was sure up. Several men ran from the saloon and followed the two riders down the street, and that started an exodus. A couple of minutes later, the only ones left in Fogle's Place were Fogle himself, John Fury, and the two unconscious cowboys.

Fogle put his hands on the bar and said, "Reckon I'd better go see what's going on, mister. Could be trouble."

"Did you know those two riders who went by raising such a ruckus?"

"Looked like Bob Nash and Lester Oakley. They've got a little spread north of here."

"Level-headed gents, are they?"

Fogle shrugged. "I suppose so. Don't really know 'em that well." He shifted around anxiously behind the bar. "I'd really like to hear what they've got to say."

Fury inclined his head toward the door. "Don't let me stop you."

The bartender hurried out. Taking his time, savoring the peace and quiet at last, Fury drank the rest of his beer, then left the empty glass on the bar and walked out to the street. Glancing to his left, he saw a crowd of people gathered in the street a couple of blocks away, in front of the town's biggest hotel. He started in that direction.

As Fury approached, he saw that the two men who had just ridden into town were at the center of the crowd. People had come not only from the saloon but also from the hotel, Ezra's diner, Drummond's Mercantile, and several other buildings to see what was causing all the uproar.

The horses the two men had ridden into town were standing at the hitch rack, heads down, sweated, sides heaving. They had been run hard. Their owners were sitting on the steps leading up to the hotel's porch, seemingly just as breathless as their mounts.

"Lester and I chased them savages, but we never could catch up to them," said one of the men. He wore a buckskin jacket and had lank, blond hair that matched the mustache drooping over his mouth. "And when we saw they had that Whitelaw girl with them, we stopped shootin' on account of we didn't want to accidentally hit her."

"Bob's tellin' it right," agreed the other man. "It pained us to let 'em go, but we figured we'd better come back here to town to spread the word that Injuns were raidin'."

"Why didn't you go on to the Whitelaw place?" asked one of the townspeople. "It was almost as close."

"Didn't think of it," replied Bob Nash.

"And like I said, we wanted to warn the town," added Lester Oakley. He was bigger and brawnier than Nash, with a beefy, clean-shaven face and curly brown hair under his farmer's hat. Both men wore holstered Colts.

"We'll get up a posse and go after them savages," another townsman said. "Maybe if we catch them in time, we can save Felicia Whitelaw."

"What about the Rangers?" asked another man. "Shouldn't we send somebody over to Fort Fisher to alert them?"

"That's a good idea," Nash said. "But I don't think we ought to wait for the Rangers to turn out. We'll send somebody to carry the word to 'em while we're goin' after those redskins."

"What kind were they, Bob?" a man called.

Nash shook his head. "Never got close enough to tell. Could've been Wacos, Cherokees . . . even Comanche."

Fury had listened long enough. With every passing minute, the Indians who had abducted that girl—Felicia Whitelaw—were getting farther and farther away. He shouldered his way to the front of the crowd surrounding Nash and Oakley and asked, "Where did this happen?"

The men looked up at him, frowning a little because he was a stranger. "Out west of here on the Brazos road," said Nash.

"Maybe three miles out of town," said Oakley.

Fury nodded and turned away. His dun was still saddled and waiting at the hitch rack in front of Fogle's. The horse had had some rest and some water from the trough beside the rail. It could handle another ride.

Behind him, Fury heard low-voiced conversation and knew the crowd was muttering about how he was the hombre who had just knocked out Billy and Judd in a fist fight. Several men hurried after him.

Among them were Nash and Oakley, who came striding up beside him. "You goin' after them savages?" asked Nash.

"You said they took a girl prisoner," Fury replied. That was all that needed to be said as far as he was concerned.

"And killed her brother, too," Oakley said. "They're a mean bunch, mister."

"I'll remember that," Fury said dryly.

He had fought Indians all along the Santa Fe Trail, had scouted with Kit Carson and Fremont, had battled both against and alongside several of the tribes that rode the Great Plains. For the most part, Fury respected the Indians he had encountered and even liked some of them. But that didn't mean he would stand by idly while a band of them murdered a man and rode off with a female prisoner.

"We'll go with you," said Nash. "Just let us get a couple of fresh horses. Show you right where it happened."

Fury nodded. "There a sheriff around here?" he asked.

Oakley shook his head. "Nope. Only law's the Rangers, and they're a couple miles downriver at Fort Fisher."

"I'll wait while you switch your saddles," Fury told the two men, "but only for a few minutes."

Nash and Oakley turned back, as did the other men who had followed Fury. They scurried for their horses, running home to fetch rifles, shotguns, and handguns as well. Before five minutes had passed, a formidable group of well-armed, mounted men had formed in the street near the hotel. One of them was sent galloping downriver to alert the Rangers to the Indian raid, while the others rode west along the Brazos.

Nash and Oakley led the group while Fury rode along just behind them. Night had fallen, leaving only a faint line of red along the western horizon toward which they rode. The stars had popped out, though, and a three-quarter moon was rising in the east, giving the riders enough light to easily follow the trail beside the river. Several men carried torches they had gotten from the general store, pitch-soaked cloth wrapped around short lengths of wood. The torches would be lit when the posse reached the scene of the Indian attack.

As they rode, Fury considered the possibility that the ambush was just a diversionary tactic. The Indians could have killed the Whitelaw boy and grabbed his sister just to draw a sizable group of men out of town, then a larger band could swoop in and attack the settlement itself. It was possible but not likely, Fury decided. Waco was a good-sized town with a Ranger post nearby. Even with this makeshift posse gone, there would be plenty of defenders left in town, and the Indians would know that if they had a lick of sense.

No, he figured, this was an isolated raid—a bunch of young bucks out looking for some excitement, rather than the start of serious hostilities.

Of course, even if that was the case, it wouldn't make a damn bit of difference to Felicia Whitelaw and her brother. The boy was still dead, and Felicia . . .

Well, Felicia might soon wish she was.

CHAPTER
4

....

The moonlight was bright enough for Fury to spot the abandoned buggy before the men from Waco reached it. The horse was moving around nervously in its traces, obviously still spooked by what had happened and by the scent of death coming from the huddled shape on the ground nearby.

The posse members reined in, and the men carrying torches used flint and tinderboxes to strike sparks and light them. The torches flared up, casting a garish yellow-red illumination over the grisly scene.

The bloodstains on Joshua Whitelaw's shirt had dried to a dark brown that was almost black. Fury's mouth tightened into a grim line as he looked down at the pale, lifeless young face. Joshua hadn't been much over twenty years of age, a grown man out here on the frontier, but still too damned young to die as far as Fury was concerned.

He reached out, took one of the torches from a man next to him. Urging the dun forward, Fury studied the tracks in the dust of the trail, and the marks there confirmed the story Nash and Oakley had told. During the ride out here, they had given him more of the details, including the way that Joshua had appeared to be trying to outrun the Indians back into town. The way the buggy was turned supported that, too.

In the welter of marks on the road, Fury picked out the tracks of quite a few unshod ponies. The tracks headed southwest, veering away from the river. Once the riders had left the road, their trail became harder to follow on the new crop of spring grass.

"They headed off over that hill," Nash said, pointing to a dark bulk about half a mile away. "Lester and I chased them part of the way, then dropped back and headed for town."

"Didn't want to ride into an ambush," admitted Oakley, sounding somewhat ashamed of himself.

Nobody here was going to blame the two of them for not pursuing the raiders any farther, though. It had taken courage to confront the Indians in the first place.

Fury glanced over his shoulder at the rising moon. "I'll trail along after them for a while," he grunted. He heeled the dun into a trot, heading for the hill where the Indians had disappeared.

After a few seconds, the rest of the men rode after him.

Likely none of them knew it, but the man they were following was probably the best tracker in several hundred miles; they would have had to go clear out to the New Mexico Territory and hunt up Kit Carson to find a better one. Fury's keen eyes roved the ground in the pale wash of moonlight, spotting signs that nine out of ten men would have missed.

And despite that, less than an hour later he had to admit that he had lost the trail.

That wasn't surprising, Fury thought as he reined in and wearily leaned forward in the saddle, resting his hands on the saddlehorn. Tracking at night was always a tricky proposition. Tracking Indians at night was next to impossible. He looked at the other men and shook his head. "Sorry."

"Hell, mister, nobody really expected you to be able to follow 'em," one of the townies said.

"That's right," added another man. "We'd better head back to the river and ride over to the Whitelaw place. Somebody's got to tell Preston and Muriel what's happened."

Bob Nash spoke up. "That's a chore I sure enough don't want, boys. Lester and me were on our way home when we came up on the trouble earlier. If it's all right with y'all, we'll be on our way."

"Sure, Bob," one of the man said. "We'll take care of it from here. Thanks for everything you and Lester did."

"It wasn't enough," Lester Oakley said in a choked voice. "It sure as hell wasn't enough."

All the men understood how he felt, but at the same time, they also knew he and Nash had done everything they could.

Fury thought about riding back to Waco and letting the other men go on to the Whitelaw ranch. He was pretty sure he could find his way back to town from here. But he had come this far; it wouldn't hurt him to stick a while longer.

Nash and Oakley rode with the other men back to the river, then swam their horses across the stream and headed north. Fury and the rest of the posse turned west, following the river road. One of the men led the horse that was pulling the buggy. Joshua Whitelaw's body had been placed back in the vehicle.

Before they reached the Whitelaw place, the sound of hoofbeats came from in front of them. The posse stopped and waited, and less than a minute later, a small group of horsemen trotted into sight. The newcomers reined up sharply when they saw the men in the road.

"Who's that?" someone called.

"That you, Jase?" replied one of the men with Fury.

"Yeah. Pres sent me and some of the boys out to look for Joshua and Felicia. They went to town this afternoon and ain't come back—" The rider's voice stopped abruptly when he saw the buggy.

"We got bad news, Jase. Joshua's been killed by Indians, and they've run off with Felicia."

"God!" The exclamation was choked out of the man called Jase. "Joshua . . . is he—"

"In the buggy. We were just heading out to the ranch to break the news to Preston and Muriel." The townsman quickly explained about the Indian attack that Nash and Oakley had tried unsuccessfully to interrupt.

Jase lifted a hand and scrubbed it over his lean face. "Lord, this is goin' to be hard on 'em," he said shakily. "Ain't no use in delayin' it, though. They've got to know." He swung his horse around, the men with him following suit, and all of them fell in with the posse from Waco.

"That's Jase Sutton," one of the townies told Fury in a quiet voice. "He's Whitelaw's foreman, been with him since before the family came from Alabama. He's known Joshua and Felicia since they were sprouts. This's got to be hard on him, too."

Fury nodded. Sudden death was a fact of life out here on the frontier, but it still wasn't something you ever got used to.

"Got any idea where they took Felicia?" asked Sutton as they rode along. Despite his grief, there was an air of practicality about the man.

One of the townies waved a hand at Fury. "This fella here followed the tracks a couple of miles. The Injuns were heading southwest."

Sutton looked over at Fury. "Don't reckon I know you, mister."

"Name's John Fury."

"Wish I could say it was a pleasure to make your acquaintance, Mr. Fury, but the way things are . . ."

"I understand," said Fury. "I reckon Whitelaw's going to want to go after his daughter."

"Pres would if he could, that's for damn sure," replied Sutton. "But a cow stepped on his foot this afternoon. It's swole up 'bout twice its normal size. I figure Pres'll be laid up for a week, maybe more." Sutton's voice hardened. "But me an' the boys'll damn sure go after those savages if Pres tells us to."

Sutton was a leathery old-timer, but Fury could hear the eagerness in his voice to go looking for the Indians who had carried off Felicia Whitelaw. The other ranch hands echoed that sentiment. Evidently Preston Whitelaw was the kind of man who inspired a great deal of loyalty in his employees.

Lamps were burning in nearly every window of the Whitelaw house when they reached it. The house was a large, two-story frame structure set in a grove of oaks. A fresh coat of whitewash made it gleam in the moonlight. Nearby ran a creek lined with cottonwoods, and behind the house were a big barn and several outbuildings. Even at night, Fury could tell it was a fine place.

The front door banged open as the group of riders came to a stop in front of the house. The lamplight that spilled through the open door showed a boy in his late teens hurrying out to meet them. "Did you find them, Jase?" he called. "Who're all those—"

Just as Sutton had done, the youngster choked off his questions at the sight of the buggy. He knew without having to ask any more that something was wrong.

Another boy, maybe a year younger, came out of the house. "What is it?" he asked. "Pa heard horses—"

Fury was starting to hate the way folks fell silent like that.

Sutton swung down from his saddle. "There's bad news, boys," he said. "Real bad news. But come on in the house, so I'll only have to say it once."

Most of the other men had dismounted, Fury among them. Sutton glanced over his shoulder and asked, "Would you come with me, Mr. Fury, since you're the one who did the trackin'?"

Fury nodded. Preston Whitelaw would want to know about the trail they had followed, even if it hadn't panned out.

The two boys crowded around Sutton as he went into the house, asking frantic questions of the old-timer. Sutton took off

his battered hat and made a curt gesture with it. "I done told you
boys just to wait 'til I'm talkin' to your pa."

The youngsters fell silent. There was a resemblance between
them, and he also saw some of the same features he had seen
on Joshua Whitelaw's dead face. He pegged them as Joshua's
younger brothers. Both of them were good-looking young men,
sturdily built with dark hair. The younger of the two was perhaps
a little more slender than his brother.

The floor of the house was built of planks rather than split-log
puncheons, and a woven rug covered the foyer just inside the
front door. A parlor with fine furniture opened up to the right,
while to the left was a dining room with a long hardwood table
polished to a high shine. The Whitelaws had money and obviously didn't mind spending it, but the quality of the furniture told
Fury that Preston Whitelaw was a man to get his money's worth.
This was a far cry from the dogtrot cabins many settlers threw up
when they came to Texas.

Down a short hallway from the foyer was a staircase leading to
the second floor. A girl of about sixteen appeared on those stairs,
an anxious look on her face. She was pretty and probably would
have been downright beautiful if she hadn't looked so worried.
Her blonde hair was pulled back in a ponytail that hung down
her back.

"Did you find them, Jase?" she called to Sutton.

He didn't answer her question, asking one of his own instead.
"Is your ma still upstairs with your pa, Laurel?"

"Yes, they're in Pa's room, but they heard you ride in, and
they're mighty worried." She frowned past Sutton at Fury and
her brothers. From her features, Fury knew she was another of
the Whitelaw offspring.

"Come on," Sutton said. He led Fury and the youngsters up the
stairs, taking the girl's arm when he reached her. Laurel Whitelaw
turned pale, sensing that some catastrophe had happened.

The group went down the second-floor hallway to a large bedroom. Inside the room was a big four-poster bed covered with a
quilted spread. Wolfskin rugs were on the floor, and on one side
of the room was a fireplace. It was definitely a man's room, with
several rifles hung up on pegs on the wall.

From the way the man sitting up in the bed fit into his surroundings, Fury knew he had to be Preston Whitelaw. He had
a stern face and a high forehead underneath thinning dark hair

shot through with gray. His eyes were brown, and Fury felt the power of their gaze when it touched on him. Whitelaw's right leg was propped on top of the covers, and the foot was swathed with bandages.

Beside him on the bed sat a middle-aged woman with blonde hair pulled into a neat bun on the back of her head. She wore a store-bought dress but had a typical homespun apron over it. She was holding Whitelaw's hand very tightly.

"What is it, Jase?" Preston Whitelaw asked in a gruff, business-like voice. Under that firm tone could be heard a tiny quiver of fear, however.

"Bad news, Pres, Muriel." Sutton's gnarled fingers bent his hat out of shape in his agitation. "We've got Joshua's body downstairs in the buggy. Injuns killed him and stole Felicia when they was on their way back from town this evenin'."

Muriel Whitelaw's free hand went to her mouth and she screamed past it. "No! Oh, dear Lord, no!" she cried.

Whitelaw's face was stony. His foot might be banged up so that he couldn't walk, but his shoulders bunched with strength as he pulled his wife around and folded her into his embrace. Murial buried her face against his chest and sobbed.

The girl Laurel was crying, too, her face covered by her hands. The two young men both looked white and shaken.

Fury felt sorry for all of them. He hadn't expected to run into trouble like this when he rode into Waco, but now he was hip-deep in it.

Sutton gestured toward him and went on, "This fella's name is John Fury. Him and some of the men from town tried to follow the tracks them savages left."

Whitelaw looked at Fury as he continued trying to comfort his wife. "Did you find anything, Mr. Fury?" he asked.

"Just that they headed southwest," replied Fury, "and I don't reckon that helps much. There's a lot of open country that way."

Whitelaw nodded slowly. "Yes, there is." He blinked and shook his head, as if unsure of what to do next, but then his stricken features firmed with determination. "Peyton, Frank, take your sister downstairs and see to her."

"Yes, Pa," the older of the two boys answered automatically. Each of them took one of Laurel's arms and led her from the room.

Whitelaw patted his wife on the back. "There, there," he said. "It'll be all right, Muriel. We'll get her back, and we'll even the score for Joshua. Just you wait and see."

That was being mighty optimistic, Fury thought, and besides, he doubted if Muriel Whitelaw gave a damn about evening the score right now. All she would want was to have her oldest daughter and son back. That was impossible as far as Joshua was concerned.

With some luck, though, Felicia might be a different story.

"Get the men ready to ride at first light, Jase," said Whitelaw. "Take as many of them as you need."

"Sure, Pres," nodded Sutton.

Whitelaw looked at Fury again. "Do you have any . . . experience at this sort of thing, Mr. Fury?"

With a shrug, Fury said, "I've tracked Indians before, if that's what you're asking. I've never gone after white prisoners, though."

"I'll want to have a talk with you later. You'll spend the night?"

Fury had planned on staying in town, but there looked to be plenty of room in the Whitelaw house. Besides, now that he had gotten mixed up in this, he wasn't ready to just ride away and leave these people to their troubles. Most of the time, he was content to mind his own business, but a man couldn't always do that.

"I'll stay," he nodded.

CHAPTER
5
. . . .

At Preston Whitelaw's suggestion, Sutton showed Fury to one of the spare bedrooms in the house. Fury would have been willing to bed down in the bunk house with the rest of the ranch hands, but Whitelaw wouldn't hear of it.

"There's plenty of room," Whitelaw said. "No need for you to stay in the bunk house, Mr. Fury."

Not wanting to argue with the man under the circumstances, Fury followed Sutton down the hall to another room. This one was considerably smaller and furnished with only a bed, a chair, and a chamber pot, but that was plenty for Fury. The bed felt comfortable when he tested it with a hand.

"Reckon you'll be goin' with us when we ride out in the mornin'," Sutton said after he had ushered Fury into the room.

"That a problem?"

Sutton shook his head. "No, sir. I'll be right glad to have somebody along who knows this country. Been less'n two years since we come here from Alabama. I've learned my way around some, but maybe not enough for a job like this. Hell of a lot different than runnin' a plantation."

"Reckon that's true," grunted Fury.

"I'll fetch you when Pres is ready to talk to you again. You had your supper?"

Fury nodded. "Back in Waco."

"You want anything to eat or drink, there's whiskey downstairs in the parlor and a cookshack out back. You can rustle for yourself or get my wife to fix somethin' for you. We live in that cabin next to the bunk house."

"I'll be fine," Fury assured him.

Sutton stuck out a hand. "Thanks for pitchin' in, Mr. Fury.

This's a bad time, mighty bad, and I 'spose we can use all the help we can get."

"Glad I was around," said Fury, shaking hands with the old foreman.

That was only half-true, Fury thought when Sutton was gone. If he had never even heard about this trouble, he could be back in Waco resting up a little before pushing on. There were bad things going on all over the place; he didn't hear about most of them, and he didn't feel guilty about them. Man couldn't take on all the troubles of the world, Fury had told himself more than once as he drifted along the frontier.

Somehow he wound up taking on more than his share, though. What he ought to do was find him a woman and a piece of ground and settle down on it, raise some kids and maybe some horses.

He would never do it, though. Fury was as sure of that as he was of anything in the world.

He was lying on the bed, thinking those thoughts and looking up at the ceiling in the light of a small candle in a holder on the wall, when a knock came on the door. Fury had taken off his gunbelt and hung it on the back of the chair, right beside the bed. He rolled off the straw mattress now, his hand going to the butt of the Dragoon Colt out of habit. He paused. Not likely he'd need a gun under these conditions.

Fury stood up, went to the door, opened it without asking who was there. He had a feeling he knew.

Preston Whitelaw stood in the corridor wearing a robe belted tightly around his waist. He wore a slipper on his uninjured foot. In his hand was clutched a heavy walking stick, and he leaned on it as he said, "We'll have that talk now, Mr. Fury, if it's all right with you."

Stepping back to let his host into the room, Fury said, "I would have come down the hall to see you."

Whitelaw shook his head. "Finally got my wife to sleep, and I don't want anything bothering her. Besides, you're the one doing me the favor. I should come to you."

"You're talking about me riding with your men to try to find your daughter?"

"Of course." Whitelaw lowered himself onto the straight-backed chair, while Fury sat on a corner of the bed. "You know I appreciate what you're doing."

"Haven't done anything yet," said Fury with a shake of his

head, "except lose the trail of those Indians."

"You'll find it again in the morning," said Whitelaw, trying to sound confident. He regarded Fury intently and went on, "I intend to see that you're well paid for your efforts on behalf of my family, sir."

Fury had figured that offer would be forthcoming. He didn't like to take advantage of somebody else's misfortune, but on the other hand, his funds were pretty low right now. He had enough money to get on down to San Antonio, but then he would have needed to find some kind of job. San Antonio was a hell of a nice place in the spring, he recalled, especially if you had plenty of money in your pockets when you got there. Good food, pretty *senoritas*, and enough time to laze around under the trees along the winding little San Antonio River. There were a hell of a lot worse ways to pass a few weeks—or months.

But he wasn't going to take Whitelaw's money under false pretenses. "There's no way I can guarantee we'll get your daughter back, Mr. Whitelaw," he said.

"I know that," replied the rancher. "But you're going to try, and that's worth something. Hell, that's worth a lot." He stared down at his foot and added bitterly, "I'd be going myself if I wasn't so damned clumsy."

"Cow can take a man by surprise every now and then."

Whitelaw nodded. "I think I could probably ride, no matter what Jase says. He's nothing but an old mother hen."

"Better you should stay here and take care of your wife," Fury told him. "She's going to have it mighty rough for a while."

"Yes. Women remember too much, like . . . like when Joshua was a baby, and Felicia, too. To Muriel, those times seem like just . . . yesterday."

Whitelaw stood up sharply and limped toward the door, his face turned away from Fury. Fury respected that and stayed where he was.

With his back still turned, Whitelaw paused at the door and said, "I won't insult you by talking any more about money, sir. Just know that I'll be in your debt, and Preston Whitelaw always pays his debts. Sleep well, Mr. Fury. You'll be getting an early start."

Under the circumstances, Fury doubted he would sleep much at all, but there was no need to tell Whitelaw that.

"I'll be ready to ride," was all he said.

• • •

As Fury had expected, his sleep was restless. The bed was almost *too* comfortable, and that could throw somebody who was accustomed to sleeping in a bedroll on the ground most of the time, with a saddle for a pillow.

When Jase Sutton rapped quietly on Fury's door about an hour before dawn, Fury was already up and fully dressed, his mental alarm having roused him in plenty of time. He opened the door and stepped out into the corridor, wearing his gunbelt and holding his hat.

"Mornin'," said Sutton.

"Good morning."

The foreman shrugged. "Don't know how good it is yet. Reckon the day'll tell the story."

Fury nodded in understanding.

Together they went down to the dining room and found the long table nearly full. All of Whitelaw's ranch hands were there, along with the rancher himself and his two sons. Laurel Whitelaw and an older woman Fury took to be Sutton's wife were serving the cowboys, carrying in platters of bacon, ham steaks, biscuits, scrambled eggs, and flapjacks. Fury and Sutton took the remaining empty chairs at Whitelaw's left, across from his sons Peyton and Frank. Both young men looked solemn, as did their father. Laurel was too busy, her face flushed from the work and the heat of the cookshack, to be dwelling on the family's losses. There was no sign of Muriel Whitelaw, and Fury assumed she was still in bed.

"Good morning, Mr. Fury," Whitelaw greeted him. "Sleep well?"

"Well enough," lied Fury.

"Good. Dig in. There's plenty of food. We set a good table here."

"Yes, sir, you surely do," Fury agreed. Whitelaw had a brisk, businesslike air about him this morning. Probably that was the only way he could keep himself from thinking too much about what had happened.

Fury helped himself as the platters were passed around, and Laurel brought a coffeepot and filled his cup for him. He had more of an appetite than he would have expected and was able to finish off all the food he heaped on his plate. Laurel refilled his coffee cup twice during the meal.

There wasn't much conversation around the table. The ranch hands seemed to be just as subdued as Peyton and Frank Whitelaw. When the meal was over and everyone stood up, Fury saw that the two youngsters were each wearing a holstered revolver. Looked like they planned on coming along with the rescue party.

That thought brought a slight frown to Fury's face. It wasn't that he disliked or distrusted the Whitelaw boys. It was just that they were mighty young for a job like this. Whether he wanted to or not, he would wind up watching out for them, and that could be dangerous for everybody else in the group. On the other hand, he himself had been out on his own by the time he was their age, surviving in a pretty rugged world. Maybe he was underestimating Peyton and Frank.

Nearly everyone went outside, even Whitelaw, limping along in the forefront of the group, in fact. Laurel and Mrs. Sutton were the only ones who stayed behind. They began to clear off the table.

Preston Whitelaw went over to a wicker chair on the front porch of the house and lowered himself into it, lifting his foot to prop it on the porch railing. It should have been a leisurely posture, but Whitelaw still made it look as if he was a coiled spring ready to pop. "Have some of the boys get the horses ready to go, Jase," he said.

"Yes, sir." Sutton motioned to several of the hands, who headed at a trot for the barn and the big corrals beyond.

Whitelaw looked toward the river. In this pre-dawn light, the stream itself wasn't visible, but the trees that marked its course were beginning to stand out from the shadows. A lantern was lit and hung from the ceiling of the porch, casting a yellow half-circle of light into the yard in front of the house. The air outside was cool, almost cold.

"The sun should be up by the time you reach the place where the trail petered out," Whitelaw commented to Fury. "Maybe you'll have good luck in picking it up again."

"All we can do is try," Fury said.

Suddenly, one of the cowboys said, "Riders comin', Mr. Whitelaw."

The rancher leaned forward in his chair and peered down the trail to the east. Fury did likewise. He could hear the hoofbeats now; it sounded like quite a few riders were approaching. Some of the townspeople from Waco, maybe, come to help Whitelaw's men search for Felicia?

As the group of horsemen rode into the yard, Fury saw that guess was wrong. These men were no simple townies. All of them had a rangy, hard-bitten look about them. They were well armed, and they rode good horses. Their leader waved them to a stop, then walked his horse right up to the porch, so that he could peer over the railing directly at Preston Whitelaw.

"Mornin', Mr. Whitelaw," he said. He glanced at the men gathered on the porch. "Looks like you've got your boys ready to ride."

"Damn right," snapped Whitelaw. "What business is that of yours, Captain?"

"Reckon you know what business it is of mine. It's the Rangers' job to go after them Injuns what stole your daughter. Your boys'd just get in our way. I'd appreciate it if you'd keep 'em at home."

So these strangers were a troop of Texas Rangers, thought Fury. He remembered that someone had taken word of the tragedy to their local headquarters, Fort Fisher.

"What am I supposed to do, then, Sprague?" Whitelaw asked angrily. "Just sit back and wait?"

The Ranger captain called Sprague nodded. "That's right."

Sprague was in his forties, Fury guessed, a well-built man with broad shoulders who looked at home in the saddle. His features were lined and craggy. He sported a short salt-and-pepper beard and had blue eyes narrowed in a perpetual squint that told of a lifetime spent outdoors. A black hat sat on his head, and he wore a blue and gray striped shirt with a black vest over denim pants. There was a Ranger badge—a five-pointed star set inside a silver circle—pinned to his vest, but he was the only one of the troop who wore such a badge. Just looking at Sprague, Fury sensed that the man would be plenty tough, even mean, when he thought he had to be.

His face taut with anger, Whitelaw started to push himself up out of his chair, but Jase Sutton's hand on his shoulder stopped him. "Don't go gettin' riled up, Pres," the foreman cautioned. "Won't do no good."

Whitelaw sank back in his chair, but his face didn't lose any of its anger. "Listen, Sprague, I'm not one of your Rangers," he said. "You can't give orders to me."

"The hell I can't," shot back Sprague. "Me an' my men are the law around here, Whitelaw. You'd do well to remember that."

"We can't go against the law, Pres," Sutton said quietly.

Sprague leaned forward in his saddle and regarded Whitelaw intently. "Maybe I spoke a mite too rough. Reckon I know how you feel, Whitelaw. If I had a daughter and she was grabbed by Injuns, I'd want to go after her, too, or at least send my men after her. But dealin' with the Injun threat is the Rangers' job. You know that."

Whitelaw said bitterly, "I know that if you have a full-scale battle with those Indians, Felicia's liable to wind up dead."

"Well, we'll do everything we can to see that don't happen," promised Sprague.

Whitelaw sighed. "All right. Like Jase says, we can't go against the law—at least not yet. I'll give you a chance, Captain. But if you don't bring my daughter back, I'll take things into my own hands, regardless of the consequences. I can promise you that."

"Fair enough," said Sprague with a curt nod. "If you'll just tell us where we can pick up the trail . . ."

"I'll do better than that." Whitelaw gestured at Fury, who was standing with one shoulder leaned negligently against a porch pillar. "This man can show you."

Sprague looked over at Fury and paid attention to him for the first time. He frowned. "Don't recall seein' you around town, mister. Who are you?"

"I just got into Waco yesterday. Name's Fury."

"And you can show us the trail?"

Fury nodded.

"Well, I reckon that wouldn't hurt," Sprague said grudgingly. "You ready to ride?"

Fury saw that one of the ranch hands had led his dun out of the barn and was holding its reins. The horse was saddled and a little frisky this morning, ready to get out and do some work. "I'm ready," said Fury.

"Come on, then. I ain't promisin' how far you'll go with us, though."

Fury didn't say anything as he mounted up. No point in causing another argument with the Ranger captain just yet.

He intended to go the whole way.

CHAPTER
6

. . . .

Since he was going to be showing them the trail, Fury rode at the head of the Rangers, next to Captain Sprague. As he jogged the dun along the river road, he was aware that Sprague was studying him with more than a casual interest.

"Seems like I've heard your name before," the captain finally said.

Fury shrugged. "Reckon I'm not the only one who's got it."

"Front handle wouldn't be John, would it?"

"It would."

Sprague nodded. "Figured as much. Been in a scrape or two, ain't you?"

"I'm not wanted, if that's what you mean. There's no paper out on me. Any fights I've been in, I reckon I've been on the right side."

The Ranger chuckled, but it wasn't a friendly sound. "Right side, wrong side, that's just a matter of luck. Maybe you were on the side that won, but that don't make you better'n any other gunman."

Fury kept a tight rein on his temper. "Like I said, I'm not wanted. And right now, you need me, Captain, to show you which way those Indians went."

"Yeah, I reckon. Likely we could find the trail ourselves, but you might save us some time. An' time's probably mighty important to that Whitelaw gal right now."

Sprague was right about that, thought Fury. The longer Felicia Whitelaw was in the hands of the Indians, the greater the likelihood they would molest her, or having done that, grow tired of her and kill her. There was a better chance they would take her back to their main camp and make a slave out of her, but you could never tell what an Indian might do.

When they reached the spot where the attack had taken place, Fury pointed it out, then led the Rangers to the southwest. There

35

had been no rain and little wind the night before, so many of the tracks he had followed then were still visible.

After the group had ridden a mile or so along the trail, Sprague said, "We can follow this sign for ourselves. You can turn back now, Fury. Go back to Whitelaw's ranch or on into Waco, whatever you want. Just stay out of trouble."

Fury didn't slow the dun. "I took cards in this hand, Captain. I intend to play it out."

Sprague gave him a hard glance. "You're refusin' a direct order?"

"Like Whitelaw said, I'm not under your command, mister. And I'm not breaking any law by riding here."

The Ranger's mouth was a grim, angry line in that neatly trimmed beard. After a moment's silence, he said, "Suit yourself. But if there's trouble, you're on your own. We ain't lookin' out for you."

"Fine by me," Fury told him.

There was no more talk between them until they reached the spot where Fury had lost the trail the night before. Then he spoke up, and the troop of Rangers reined to a halt. Fury and Sprague walked their horses forward slowly, each man studying the ground.

They were in a valley between a couple of hogback ridges. The ground was rocky here, not the kind to take tracks easily. Fury found a few marks on a long stretch of stone that might have been made by horseshoes, but Sprague shook his head.

"Them Injun ponies'd be unshod," he said. "Besides, I reckon those tracks were made a while back."

Fury nodded. The captain had a point. He wasn't sure the tracks were as old as Sprague seemed to think, but that didn't really matter. They hadn't been made by the animals he and the Rangers were seeking.

One of the other men let out a yell and pointed to some tracks he found leading northwest. "Those are unshod horses," he said.

Fury rode over and swung down from his saddle, going to a knee to study the marks the man had found. Sprague joined him, and a moment later the disgusted grunt from the Ranger captain told Fury that Sprague had come to the same conclusion he had.

"Must be a band of wild mustangs," said Sprague. "Hoofprints aren't deep enough for those ponies to've been carryin' anybody."

Fury nodded. "That's what I thought, too. Looks like we we've run into a dead end, Captain."

"Not yet," insisted Sprague. "Let's do some more lookin'."

Several more hours of searching yielded the same results, however, even though the troop of Rangers spread but across the entire valley.

The trail was gone.

Sprague took off his hat, ran his fingers through his hair, looked like he wanted to smash the hat down on the ground in frustration. Fury didn't help matters by asking, "What now, Captain?"

"What now?" echoed Sprague. "I'll tell you what now. We're goin' to find out what happened to that girl."

"How?" Fury asked bluntly.

"Them Wacos'll know. Hell, they might even have her there in their village. I'll just bet that's what they did. They rode off this way to throw us off the scent, then circled back around toward town."

Fury frowned. Sprague had come up with this theory off the top of his head, and Fury didn't put much credence in it. The Waco Indians, from what he knew of them, didn't want trouble with the whites. And yet there was just enough of a possibility that Sprague was right to warrant checking it out. They sure as hell weren't doing any good wandering around out here.

Sprague waved the Rangers back toward the Brazos. Fury rode with them. There was nothing else he could do except stick with the Rangers as Whitelaw's representative. When the group of riders reached the river, they turned east toward the settlement.

The village of the Waco Indians was now west of the town to which they had given their name. The Indians had been crowded out by the arrival of the white men, and while the Wacos could be plenty warlike when it came to their relations with other tribes, evidently they had sensed early the futility of trying to oppose the spread of white settlement. Other than a few minor incidents, they had always gotten along well with the white men.

That could change, though, Fury knew. The murder of Joshua Whitelaw and the kidnapping of his sister could be the first signs of a new attitude among the Wacos.

The village was a little south of the main road that ran beside the river. Sprague, Fury, and the Rangers veered toward it. Fury saw the dome-shaped lodges made of bent saplings and covered with grass and dried mud. Beyond those lodges were cultivated fields where the spring planting was going on. The Wacos were good hunters, from what Fury had heard, but they didn't mind tilling the soil, either.

The village's dogs sent up a racket as Fury and the Rangers rode in. Children popped out of the lodges to watch the white men on big horses. The mothers of those youngsters were just as curious. Several men came loping in hurriedly from the fields to see what was going on. One of them, a slender man in buckskins, headed straight for Captain Sprague.

"Why have the Rangers come to the village of the Waco?" he asked in passable English as he strode over to Sprague's horse and looked up at the captain. He moved like a young man, but Fury saw now that he was middle-aged, probably the chief of this band.

Fury wasn't expecting what Sprague did next. The Ranger lifted his right foot from the stirrup, planted it in the chest of the Indian who had asked him what they were doing here, and shoved. The Indian staggered back several feet before he tripped and fell. He landed in the dust and glared at Sprague, who calmly drew his Colt and leveled it at the man.

"I want some answers," growled Sprague. "Where's that girl, and why'd you kill her brother?"

Fury had tensed in his saddle at the first sign of violence. The Indians reacted as might be expected after an attack on their leader. Those holding shovels and hoes tightened their grips on the tools, tools that might easily become weapons. Others shifted their hands to the knives they wore.

But the Rangers in Sprague's troop evidently knew their captain well. Before the Waco chief even hit the ground, the rest of the Rangers had drawn their guns. They were outnumbered, but the advantage the revolvers gave them was more than enough. The Indians stiffened and glowered, but they made no move to attack.

The chief lifted himself to his feet and knocked dust off his buckskins. "I know nothing about this of which you speak," he said.

"Don't lie to me, redskin," said Sprague. "I know damn well some of your bucks murdered Joshua Whitelaw yesterday evenin', and you brought his sister Felicia back here to your village."

The Waco's eyes widened in surprise that looked genuine to

Fury. "If someone told you this," the man declared, "then they are lying. We live at peace with the white man. We know this man Whitelaw. He and his family are our friends."

"Hell of a way to treat your friends."

Fury could see desperation growing in the eyes of the Waco chief. Most of the Indians probably understood English and knew what Sprague was accusing them of. An anxious stirring went through the village. If this went much farther, there was going to be bloodshed. Fury could almost smell it.

"Wait a minute," he said to Sprague. "Maybe he's telling the truth."

Sprague shot a glance at him, glaring at what he took to be Fury's interference. "You ever know an Injun to tell the truth?" he asked scornfully.

"As a matter of fact," said Fury, "I've known several who were more truthful than most white men."

"Well, this buck ain't one of 'em," countered Sprague. "Stay out of this, Fury." He swung back toward the chief and lifted the pistol in his hand. "Now where's that girl?"

Fury's jaw clenched in frustration. This confrontation was liable to turn into a bloodbath the way it was going, and there didn't seem to be anything he could do to stop it.

"The Cherokee!" said the Waco suddenly. "The Cherokee must have done this evil thing."

Sprague hesitated. "You're just sayin' that 'cause the Wacos and the Cherokees ain't never got along."

"It is true we hate the Cherokee," the chief said. "But they hate the white man. You know this is so."

Everything Fury had ever heard said that the Cherokees were about in the same boat as the Wacos. They fought against each other but generally avoided conflict with the whites. Still, there might be something to what the chief said.

After a moment during which the same thoughts must have gone through Sprague's head, the Ranger captain growled, "Keep talkin'."

"The Cherokee have a village west of here, maybe two days' ride. This is where you should look for the white girl."

"Maybe. But I want to take a look around here first, just to make sure you ain't lyin' to me, boy."

It cost the chief an obvious effort of will to tolerate Sprague's insulting tone, but he waved a hand at the lodges of his people.

"Look all you wish. You will find nothing."

Sprague made a sharp gesture to his men, and several of them dismounted and spread out through the village, still holding their rifles and pistols ready for instant use if they were opposed. The Waco chief spoke loudly to the Indians in their own tongue, however, evidently telling them not to interfere with the search. Fury, Sprague, and the rest of the Rangers continued to sit tensely on their horses.

Less than a quarter hour was needed to search the village thoroughly. A lanky, sandy-haired Ranger came up to Sprague and shook his head. "Nothin', captain," he reported. "The Whitelaw girl ain't here, and there ain't no signs to show she has been."

Sprague nodded curtly. "All right, you and the rest of the boys get mounted up again. I reckon we'll take a *pasear* over to the Cherokee village." He looked at Fury. "You goin' to horn in on that, too?"

"Whitelaw wanted me to ride with you. The man fed me and gave me a place to sleep. I owe him."

"And you're damned stubborn on top of it."

Fury permitted himself a tiny smile. "So I've been told." He looked at the Waco chief and addressed the man directly for the first time. "What about the Comanches? Don't they raid over this way sometimes?"

Sprague didn't give the chief a chance to answer. "It wasn't Comanches who killed the boy and ran off with the girl. If they were out on a murder raid, I'd've heard about it 'fore now."

"Not if they just started."

Sprague shook his head. "The Comanche are too busy north an' west of here, I tell you. Too far west for this bunch to have been part of 'em."

"The captain speaks the truth," put in the chief. "We, too, would have heard if the Horse Indians were on the move."

"All right," said Fury. "I reckon we pay a visit to the Cherokee next."

"Be careful," said the chief, who had seen that Fury didn't draw his gun and disapproved of Sprague's rough tactics. "The Cherokee are lying savages."

" 'Bout like the rest of you redskins," Sprague commented. He hauled his horse around. "Come on. We're ridin'!"

CHAPTER
7
....

They had been damned lucky to come out of that encounter
without any real trouble, Fury thought as he and the Rangers rode
away from the Waco camp. He wondered if Sprague intended to
ask his questions of the Cherokee in the same manner.

Probably, decided Fury. Sprague obviously hated Indians and
didn't make any effort to hide the way he felt about them. That
could cause some real problems.

Fury's pack mule and his supplies were back in Waco, the
mule having been hurriedly stabled before he rode out with the
townspeople. Whitelaw could have outfitted him with some provisions, but when he'd left that morning, no one had thought
about the possibility that he might be out overnight. His bedroll was tied behind the dun's saddle, though, and these Rangers
always rode prepared. They would share their coffee and beans
with him, as well as whatever meat they brought down when
they made evening camp. The midday meal was jerky and hard-
tack gnawed in the saddle. Hell on the teeth, but it kept a man
going.

The Waco chief had said the Cherokee camp was two days'
ride west of the settlement. That might be true, but late that afternoon, Sprague suddenly reined in, held up a hand to bring the
others to a halt, and pointed ahead of them.

"Smoke," he said. "Looks like several cookin' fires."

Fury had spotted the smoke a couple of seconds before the
Ranger. He agreed with Sprague's assessment. From the looks
of the smoke, there was a good-sized camp up ahead.

"That trail we were following earlier was headed in this general direction before it petered out," Fury said.

Sprague nodded slowly. "Yeah, reckon it was." He glanced
over at Fury. "How 'bout takin' a look with me?"

"Sure."

Turning in his saddle, Sprague said to his sandy-haired lieutenant, "You're in charge while we're gone, Proctor. Stay here
unless you hear shootin'. Then you an' the boys come a-runnin'."

"You bet, Cap'n," the man grinned back at Sprague.

Sprague put his horse into an easy walk. Fury rode alongside
him. There were a couple of small hills between them and the
smoke, so they had to take the long way around to avoid being
highlighted against the sky. At last they came to a long ridge. The
smoke rose just on the other side of the slope.

"We'll leave the horses here," whispered Sprague as he swung
down. Fury followed suit. The wind was in their faces, bringing
the tang of woodsmoke with it and carrying their own smell and
that of their horses away from the Indian camp.

Moving slowly and carefully, Fury and Sprague started up
the ridge. It was thick with buffalo grass and dotted with cedars
and junipers. Before they reached the top, both men took off
their hats, went to their hands and knees, and crawled the last
few yards.

Fury peered over the crest of the ridge. The slope fell away
sharply on the other side, dropping to a small creek that trickled
over a sandy bottom. On the other side of the stream was a grassy
meadow and then a stand of oak trees. In that meadow, between
the creek and the trees, were camped about twenty braves. They
wore buckskins, but unlike the Waco, their heads were shaved
except for scalplocks that were decorated with feathers. They
had three cooking fires going and were roasting rabbits over the
flames.

Over the years, Fury had run into several Cherokees and knew
their sad story. Once one of the greatest Indian nations, respected
throughout the southeastern states where they had made their
home for centuries, the Cherokees had run into bad luck when
gold was discovered on some of their lands in Georgia.

They had no use for the soft yellow metal. But the white men
did. It was only a matter of time until the whites were moving in,
pushing the Cherokees off their land, driving them farther and
farther west.

Once that kind of thing got started, it was hard to stop. The
government had eventually stepped in and solved the problem
with its usual efficiency and fairness, rounding up the Cherokees
who were left and marching them west to Indian Territory, north
of Texas. The trip was a hard one, and many of the Indians had

died making it. Many of the ones who were left, however, had settled on the reservations given to them and regained at least a portion of their former dignity and standing among the various tribes. Some had spread out from Indian Territory, including the ones who had drifted here into central Texas and clashed with the Wacos. The band that Fury and Sprague watched now was unmistakably Cherokee.

Sprague pointed downslope with urgency and backed in that direction. Fury followed, and when they reached the bottom of the ridge, the Ranger said, "It's them, all right. Got to be."

"I didn't see the girl anywhere," said Fury. "They don't have any lodges, no women and children. That's not the main camp."

Sprague frowned at him. "I know that. That's a war party. They're the ones went out on that murder raid."

"Looked more like a hunting party to me. They're not painted for war."

"Maybe not right now. But you can take my word for it," insisted Sprague. "They're out after blood—white man's blood!" He wheeled around and reached for his horse's reins.

Fury put a hand on his arm to stop him. "Where are you going?"

"Back to get the rest of the boys, so we can put a stop to this right here and now." Sprague looked down meaningfully at Fury's hand. "I don't cotton to bein' grabbed like that, mister. You move that hand, or you an' me'll have somethin' to settle later, after we've taken care of them Injuns."

Fury released Sprague's arm, not out of any fear of the Ranger but because he wanted to try again to get through to the man. "You saw it as well as I did," he said. "Felicia Whitelaw isn't with them."

"Then they've sent her on to their main village, I reckon. I intend to find out for sure." Sprague gripped the saddlehorn and swung up. "You can come with me or stay here, whatever you want. I don't give a damn. But don't even think about warnin' those Injuns, Fury. I'll string you up to the highest cottonwood I can find if you do, and there ain't a man in Texas who'd say I was wrong to do it."

Given all the Indian trouble the settlers down here had endured, Fury knew Sprague was right. He would just have to bide his time and hope the Ranger would be reasonable and not cause another incident like the one with the Wacos.

"I'll stay here and keep an eye on them," he said. "Maybe they've got the girl back in the trees. I'll see if I can spot her."

Sprague nodded. "Good idea." He turned the horse and rode off, keeping the animal at a walk until he was far enough away that galloping hoofbeats would not be heard.

Fury left the dun where it was and climbed the ridge again. The sun was nearly down, and the light was already fading in the little valley on the other side of the creek. Fury squinted against the red rays and tried to penetrate the shadows under the trees. If Felicia was in there somewhere, she was well hidden.

He could hear the voices of the Cherokee braves as they talked and laughed among themselves. All of them seemed relaxed, not at all the way they would be acting if they were a war party. Sprague was wrong about them; there was no two ways about it. When the Ranger got back with the rest of the men, Fury intended to ask Sprague if he could ride down there first, alone, to parley with the braves. They'd come closer to finding out what they wanted to know that way than if the entire group of armed men rode in and acted threatening.

Fury waited impatiently. The sun had slipped below the horizon now, and night would be closing in soon. What the hell had happened to Sprague?

The sudden splashing was the first warning Fury had that something was wrong.

His gaze jerked to the left to search for the source of the unexpected noise, and as he came up on his knees, he heard the crack of gunshots followed by whoops and shouts. Down below, at the far end of the ridge, the troop of Texas Rangers led by Sprague charged across the creek and galloped toward the Cherokee braves, firing as they came.

Damn! Sprague had double-crossed him, leaving him here while he went back and set up an attack with the rest of the Rangers. Fury came to his feet and pulled his own gun, but there was nothing he could do with it. He wasn't going to join the ambush, but he couldn't bring himself to fire at the Rangers, either. They were just following Sprague's orders.

The Cherokees hadn't even had sentries out, Fury realized. That was how convinced they were that everything around them was peaceful at the moment. Being taken by surprise this way, they were limited in how much of a fight they could put up.

Sprague and the Rangers swept up to the camp, dropping several of the Indians with their first volley. The Walker and Dragoon Colts and even a few old Patersons continued to boom. Indians were knocked off their feet and sent sprawling by the heavy lead balls. A few of the Cherokees managed to grab their rifles—old muskets, for the most part—and get off a few shots at the attackers, but the resistance wasn't enough to blunt the force of the charge. The Rangers galloped through the camp, firing left and right and riding right over some of their victims.

"Leave some alive!" bellowed Sprague, the command clearly audible to Fury at the top of the ridge. "Don't kill 'em all!"

Sprague wanted prisoners to question, Fury figured, but that wouldn't stop him from killing most of the braves. The firing was dying away now, the battle nearly over almost before it got started. Fury holstered his gun and began to slide down the ridge toward the creek.

Below him, one of the braves splashed across the stream and started up, fleeing from the whooping, shooting Rangers. The Indian had taken only a few steps when he glanced up and saw the white man coming toward him. He let out a cry of rage, whipped an arrow from the quiver he had grabbed up when the fighting started, and fitted it to the string of his bow.

"Wait!" yelled Fury, seeing what was about to happen.

The Cherokee ignored him. Fury dove to the side as the Indian loosed the arrow. He heard it cut through the air next to him and clatter against the rocky slope. The quick move made Fury's feet slip out from under him. His balance deserted him, and he tumbled several yards before he caught himself.

He looked up to see the Indian lunging at him in the dusk. The brave had thrown aside his bow and arrows, and now a knife was clutched in his upraised right hand. The blade drove down at Fury.

Fury rolled desperately away from the striking knife. His heart was pounding, and his mouth tasted like metal. He twisted away as the Indian slashed at him again. Fury reached and grabbed with his left hand, and his fingers closed over the knife wrist of the Indian. Fury locked his elbow, keeping the backhanded cut away from him. It was awkward, fighting like this on such a steep slope, and Fury knew he'd better end this as soon as he could. Otherwise, the Cherokee would get lucky and find his flesh with that blade.

With his right hand, Fury palmed out the Dragoon. Maybe in the bad light, the Indian wouldn't see it coming. Keeping his finger out of the trigger guard to prevent an accidental shot, Fury gripped the butt of the pistol and slammed its long heavy barrel against the side of his opponent's head. The Cherokee grunted in pain, and his fingers loosened on the knife. It slid out of his hand.

Fury shoved him away, rolled over, and came to his feet. He trained the gun on the Indian, but the brave was too stunned by the blow to put up any more fight. He lay there moaning and moving around a little.

Aware now that the shooting had come to an end, Fury glanced down and saw Sprague riding into the stream and looking up at him. "See you got you one," called the Ranger captain. "Bring him on down here."

A little breathless, his pulse still racing with a mixture of fear and anger, Fury reached down, grasped the Indian's shirt, and hauled him to his feet. "Go on," he said.

The Cherokee stumbled down to the creek and across it, followed closely by Fury. Most of his fellow braves were sprawled lifelessly around the clearing. Several of the Rangers had a knot of prisoners huddled together on the bank of the stream. Fury prodded his captive over to join the others, then swung around to face Sprague.

"Goddamn you!" Fury said to the captain. "You lied to me."

"Nope." Sprague shook his head. "I said I was goin' back to get the rest of the boys, and that's just what I done. Didn't say what we were goin' to do when we got here."

"Look around," Fury said coldly. "Do you see Felicia Whitelaw?"

Sprague glanced around the once-peaceful camp and shook his head. "Just because she ain't here now don't mean this ain't the bunch that took her. Like I said, they've sent her on to their main village."

"You've got no proof of that."

"Well, let's just get us some proof." Sprague got down from his horse and stalked over to the prisoners. He put his hands on his hips, glowered at the Cherokees, and said, "Last night you bucks jumped a white man and woman in a buggy up by the Brazos. You killed the man and took off with the gal. Where is she?"

For a long moment, none of the half-dozen or so captives made any reply. Then one of them looked at Sprague and said in halting English, "This is not true. We not do this thing."

"The hell you say!" snorted Sprague. "I know you damned red heathens are responsible."

The spokesman for the Cherokees shook his head. "No, not us. Probably Wacos!"

"Yeah, that's just what they said. But we searched their village and didn't find the girl."

"No girl here!"

Sprague sighed heavily. "Like I done told you, I know you must've sent her on with a couple of bucks."

"No!" insisted the Cherokee. "We hunt, take meat back to village!"

"Cap'n . . ." One of the other Rangers had been poking around in the trees and now he came back out scratching his head in the faint light from the cooking fires. "From the looks of it, they been smokin' some meat. They got a bunch of it hung up in the trees to keep it away from varmints."

Sprague turned sharply toward the man. "Any sign of the Whitelaw girl?"

"No, sir, 'fraid not."

A grimace drew Sprague's lips away from his teeth. The evidence, what little there was of it, supported everything the Cherokee brave had said.

"He's telling the truth," Fury said quietly, his voice cold. "They didn't have a damn thing to do with what happened to Joshua and Felicia Whitelaw."

"Yeah, maybe."

"Dammit, Sprague, open your eyes!"

Sprague whipped around to face Fury. "My eyes *are* open. They been open for a long time, and they seen plenty of white folks tortured and murdered by stinkin' Injuns just like this. So don't expect me to shed any tears over these red bastards." He shouldered past Fury and started walking toward the horses. Without turning around, he ordered, "Kill the rest of 'em."

Fury lunged after him and grabbed his shoulder, spinning him around. "What?"

Sprague's gun came up and the barrel dug into Fury's breastbone. The captain's thumb was on the hammer, holding it back ready to fall. "Stay out of this, Fury," he rasped, then called to his men, "I said kill 'em!"

"You can't do that," whispered Fury. "It's murder, plain and simple."

"They've done murder, them and all their bloody-handed kinfolk. Told you I'd seen plenty of white folks killed by savages, Fury. Two of 'em were my ma and pa. Another one was my brother. And three more—my wife and our young'uns." Sprague's voice quivered with barely controlled rage. "So don't you go tellin' me one damn thing about Injuns, Fury. I know all I need to. And so do my boys. Ain't a one of 'em who ain't been through the same thing." He looked past Fury, nodded, said quietly now, "Do it."

Fury didn't turn around. He heard the yells, the sudden sounds of struggle, the brief flurry of gunshots. Then everything was quiet again as full darkness settled over the Texas hills. Fury's face was carved in lines as hard as those stony ridges.

Sprague stepped away from Fury and holstered his gun. "Come on," he said. "We've got more ridin' to do."

CHAPTER
8

· ·

Sprague wouldn't let go of his notion that Felicia Whitelaw had been taken to the main Cherokee camp, even though everything they had seen so far pointed to someone other than the Cherokees as the girl's kidnappers. Nothing would satisfy the Ranger except riding on to the Cherokee village so they could take a look at it.

Fury went with them. No matter how much he despised Sprague, that didn't change things. He had told Preston Whitelaw he would accompany the Rangers on their quest, and he intended to keep his word.

Leaving the dead braves where they had fallen, the Rangers moved on and found another spot to camp on the same creek. They might be able to put the killings out of their thoughts now that the corpses were out of sight, but it wasn't that easy for Fury. He sat apart from the other men, his memories full of blood and death.

The feelings would fade; Fury knew that. He wasn't a callous man, but he had seen too much violence, too much death, for it to make much of a permanent impression on him. Death was one of the curses that seemed to follow him around on his wanderings.

The contempt he felt for Captain Sprague would never change, though, despite the fact that he could understand why Sprague was the way he was. Some men had a limit to how much pain they could carry around before it turned them hard and bitter and twisted . . . some just kept on living.

They were up and riding at dawn, and Sprague pushed them at a hard pace all day. Fury had little to say to the man. Sprague didn't seem to mind the quiet. He kept them moving until, at a little after four in the afternoon, they found the Cherokee town.

It was a good-sized settlement in a broad, shallow valley. Fury counted forty-three lodges when he studied the village through

49

his spyglass from a mile away. That meant between two hundred and two hundred and fifty inhabitants.

Minus those twenty dead back up the trail, of course, Fury thought grimly.

He tucked his spyglass away in his saddlebag and said to Sprague, "You go charging in there like you did with those other Indians and you'll get yourself and all your men killed."

Sprague eased himself in the saddle and looped a leg around the horn. He took a plug of chewing tobacco from his vest pocket, cut off a piece with a clasp knife, and then held out the remainder to Fury. "Chaw?"

"No thanks."

After working the stuff around between his teeth for a moment, Sprague went on, "We're not chargin' in. We'll ride up nice and polite-like and ask our questions."

"If they find out you killed all the men in that hunting party, they'll never let you ride out of there."

Sprague looked pointedly at him. "Well, then, nobody'd better say anything about that—I reckon once the killin' gets started, they won't much care who is dyin' long as he had white skin. Right?"

That was true enough. Fury couldn't say anything about the ambush without dooming himself as well. He was riding with the Rangers, and the Cherokees would include him in any retribution they carried out.

"I'm not a damned fool," grated Fury. "I don't intend to say anything."

"Good. See that you remember that."

With that, Sprague slipped his foot back in the stirrup and started his horse forward in an easy trot toward the Cherokee village.

Once again, all the kids and dogs turned out to greet them. This time, however, there were more than a few men on hand, too, and they were armed with bows and arrows, rifles, and pistols instead of shovels and hoes, as had been the case back at the Wacos's settlement. Fury felt the blood in his veins run a little colder as he rode in with the Rangers under the hard-eyed scrutiny of the Cherokee warriors.

A small group of older men pushed back the flap of hide that served as a door on one of the lodges. They strode out to meet the strangers. One man, short but powerfully built, sporting a gray scalplock, carried himself with an unmistakable air of command. He stopped and waited with crossed arms, looking coolly up at the white men.

"You the chief around here?" asked Sprague.

"I am Panther's Eye, chief of the Cherokee," replied the man. "And who are you?"

"Captain Ben Sprague of the Texas Rangers, out of Fort Fisher."

Panther's Eye nodded slowly. "I know of this place. What is your business with the Cherokee?"

"We're lookin' for a girl—a white girl—who was stolen from her family by some Indians a couple of days ago."

Panther's Eye and the other Cherokees tensed, and Fury knew they were waiting to be accused of the crime. He had to give Sprague credit, though. The Ranger might be a heavy-handed bastard most of the time, but he knew when and how to be diplomatic.

"Now I know the Cherokees wouldn't've done such a thing," Sprague went on. "You're honorable folks. But we thought you might've seen some sign of other Injuns passin' through your lands in the last day or two. Maybe you've even seen the girl."

If the Cherokees were responsible for Felicia's kidnapping, Sprague had just given them a way out. They could turn Felicia over and claim that they had rescued her from a war party of some other tribe. They could lay the blame for the atrocity on the Wacos or the Comanches. If that happened, they might hate to give up Felicia, but they could look on the whole thing as a good trick they had played on the whites.

However, Panther's Eye shook his head solemnly. "We have seen no strange Indians and no white female. But if you would like to search my village . . ." He waved a hand at the lodges around them.

Fury felt a grin plucking at his mouth. The Cherokee chieftain was a crafty old buzzard, and he had just played a trump card. So far the discussion had been restrained and polite, but if Sprague accepted the invitation to look around the village, he would be casting doubt on the word of Panther's Eye. An insult like that could open up a whole new can of worms.

Sprague forced his haggard features into something that vaguely resembled a smile. "No, that's all right, Chief," he said. "I'll sure take your word on it. I reckon we'll keep lookin'."

Fury hoped Panther's Eye wouldn't invite them to spend the night. Obviously, the hunting party hadn't been missed yet, but with every hour that went by, the likelihood increased that the Cherokees would discover what had happened. Fury wanted to put some distance between themselves and the Cherokees before that occurred.

Evidently Panther's Eye wasn't in that hospitable a mood. He nodded and raised a hand in farewell to the visitors. That was a good sign, letting all the other braves in the village know that the white men were being permitted to leave in peace.

Fury glanced at the other Rangers as they rode away from the big camp. Several of them were pale, and all of them seemed to be sweating more than the warmth of the spring day would warrant. For that matter, there was a fine sheen of perspiration on his own forehead.

Not Sprague, though. He was as cool as could be.

When they had left the Cherokee village several miles behind them, Fury brought the dun up alongside the captain's horse and asked, "Well, what are you going to do now? Are you convinced the Cherokees didn't have anything to do with that raid?"

Sprague rubbed at his bearded jaw. "I ain't convinced o' nothin'," he declared stubbornly. "But I reckon it's startin' to look like they ain't to blame."

"That leaves the Comanches or some other band of renegades."

"Yeah. An' once you head west, Texas is just too damn big to go traipsin' around lookin' for every shirt-tail bunch of redskins." Sprague sighed heavily. "I reckon until we get somethin' better to go on, we'll have to head back to Waco and hope for the best."

That meant abandoning Felicia Whitelaw to the mercies—if there were any—of her captors. It was a bitter pill for Fury to swallow, yet he understood what Sprague meant. The Indians who had taken Felicia could be anywhere from the Brazos to New Mexico Territory, and that was a hell of a lot of ground to cover. Too much for one man or even one group of men. If Felicia was seen somewhere, if word got back to Waco of her whereabouts, then the Rangers could justify sending some men after her again. But until then, there were other problems to take care of, and the Rangers had always been stretched thin as it was.

"All right," said Fury. "I guess I'll go back to Whitelaw's place and let them know. It's going to be hard news. They were hoping we'd bring Felicia back with us."

"Folks always have hope when somethin' like this happens. But it ain't often that hope pays off." Sprague hesitated, then went on, "Want me to go talk to the Whitelaws with you when we get back?"

Fury hadn't expected that offer from the man. He shook his head. "I'll handle it," he said.

"It ain't really your job," Sprague pointed out.

"Maybe not," said Fury. "But I reckon I've made it mine."

They rode until after dark, made a cold camp, and got an early start the next morning, heading out while the stars still burned overhead. Like Fury, Sprague and the others were anxious to put some more miles between them and the Cherokees. Fury wondered, too, if guilt was working on any of the Rangers. He knew there wasn't any room in Sprague for such a thing, but some of the other men might regret killing all the members of that hunting party.

If that was the case, Fury didn't see any sign of it during the next couple of days. The Rangers were hard men, and they came from an existence that was rugged at best. They weren't going to waste a lot of sympathy on Indians, not when most if not all of them had lost friends and relatives to Indian raids, as Sprague had said.

The landscape became more familiar again, and Fury realized they were covering some of the same ground they had several days earlier when they were trying to trail the raiders. They hit the Brazos between Waco and the Whitelaw ranch, and as Sprague reined in and signaled a halt to his men, he turned to Fury and asked again, "Sure you don't want me to come with you?"

"I'm sure. But thanks, anyway." The words came grudgingly to Fury. He wasn't going to forget any time soon the way Sprague had ordered those prisoners killed.

Sprague lifted his hand in a wave of farewell and turned his men eastward along the river. Fury rode west, toward Preston Whitelaw's home.

The first one to see him coming was Jase Sutton. The old foreman was in one of the fields along the river that was being plowed for a cotton crop. Sutton rode along the edges of the field, keeping an eye on the mules and men doing the plowing. When he saw Fury riding along the river trail, he whipped off his hat and slapped it against his horse's rump, sending the animal into a gallop.

Fury reined in as Sutton pounded up to him. With despairing eyes, the old man saw that he was alone. "Felicia?" Sutton asked.

Fury shook his head. "We didn't find her."

Sutton cursed bitterly and twisted the hat he still held in his hands. "We should've gone after her ourselves, 'stead of trustin' the Rangers to do it."

"That wouldn't have made any difference," Fury told him. "The trail just disappeared. We searched for her among the Wacos and the Cherokees, but neither bunch had her."

"You're sure o' that?"

"I'm sure," nodded Fury. "Captain Sprague wasn't completely convinced, but I was. And even Sprague thinks it's likely now that the Comanches have her."

"Then we'll never get her back," Sutton said bleakly. "Not never." He took a deep, shuddering breath. "Come on. We'll tell the folks."

Peyton and Frank Whitelaw were out working somewhere on the spread, but Laurel was home, and she was the one who came racing out of the house when Fury and Sutton rode up. Their faces told her everything she needed to know. Her fists went to her mouth, and sobs wracked her as she sank into one of the wicker chairs on the porch.

Her mother bustled out of the house as Fury and Sutton swung down from their horses. Laurel's crying had caught her attention, and Muriel Whitelaw knew all too well the reason for it. Fury saw the last vestiges of hope die away in her eyes, to be replaced by a sorrow that might never go away. He wanted to tell her not to give up, that there was still a chance Felicia might be found, but he knew how unlikely that was. It might be a kindness, no matter how cruel it seemed right now, to let her give up.

Fingers twisting in the apron she wore, Muriel asked, "Anything, Mr. Fury? Anything at all?"

"No, ma'am," he said quietly. "We didn't find her."

Preston Whitelaw clumped onto the porch in time to hear what Fury said. He seemed to be getting around a little better now, although he still carried the heavy walking stick. "No sign of her?" he asked.

"No, sir."

Muriel sat down on the arm of the chair where Laurel was slumped, crying. She reached out and put an arm around her daughter's shoulders, holding on tightly. She began to cry, too, and Fury wished he was somewhere—anywhere—else.

Whitelaw dragged a breath into his body. His face looked a little like a sandy bank washing away under a heavy rain. Deep lines seemed to cut themselves into his features even as Fury watched. After a moment, he said, "Thank you, Mr. Fury. Thank you for everything you've done. You said all along there were no . . . no guarantees."

"The Rangers will put the word out," Fury told him. "Folks'll know to keep an eye out for a young white girl. Somebody's bound to spot her sooner or later."

The words sounded hollow to Fury even as he spoke them. Sure, somebody might see Felicia again someday—if she was still alive. And if she was, by the time anybody found her, she'd be some buck's squaw, with a handful of squalling babies to take care of. That was if she was lucky enough to have one of her captors decide he wanted her for his own. Otherwise, as a slave, she'd be passed around among the unmarried warriors. If enough years went by, she would probably forget her English, forget she had ever been anything except a Comanche woman. That happened sometimes with white prisoners, Fury knew.

And sometimes they just lost their minds.

Whitelaw limped down off the porch and came over to Fury. He put his hand in his pocket and brought out a roll of bills. "I promised I'd pay you for your effort," Whitelaw said. He peeled off several of the bills and pressed them into Fury's hand, which hung loosely at his side. Payment was the last thing on Fury's mind at the moment, what with those two females crying on the porch and Whitelaw and Sutton looking the way they did. Without even glancing at the money, Fury stuffed it into his saddle-bag.

"I'll be in town for a day or two," he said. He swung up onto the dun and turned its head away from the Whitelaw house. He put the horse into a trot along the river road.

He wasn't sure why he had said that to Whitelaw about staying on in Waco for a few days. The town had been nothing but bad luck to him ever since he had arrived, and he wished to hell he had ridden straight through it and headed on toward Austin.

But at least he was still alive, and that was more than he could say for Joshua Whitelaw and maybe Felicia, too—and those Cherokee braves who had been unlucky enough to be hunting in the wrong place at the wrong time.

Tonight, decided John Fury, would be a damned good night to get drunk.

CHAPTER
9

························

That was exactly what Fury did. He didn't go to Fogle's Place this time; Maddie might have been there, and he was in no mood for her antics. He found an even smaller saloon, a hole-in-the-wall place where there weren't any women or poker games or trouble-seeking cowboys, just a handful of drinkers who were there for one reason and one reason alone.

To get drunk.

Problem was, it didn't help a whole lot. Even though he had never seen Felicia Whitelaw, he couldn't get the image of her out of his mind, and what he saw was mixed up with the memory of those dead Indians.

He found a room in a little hotel on Franklin Street, took off his hat, boots, and gun, and flopped on the bed to toss and turn restlessly for most of the night. When he woke up early the next morning, head pounding from a hangover, he told himself the best thing he could do would be to collect the dun and his pack mule, then ride out of Waco. Never mind that he had told Whitelaw he would be around for a little while. He wanted to put the place behind him.

Instead he went out, stopped at a restaurant, and forced himself to eat. Steak, eggs, and biscuits, washed down with a potful of black coffee, settled his stomach a little and opened his eyes more.

"Must be getting old," he muttered to himself. "Else I wouldn't be sitting around brooding like this."

"Sir?"

Fury looked up in surprise. He hadn't been aware that the plump young waitress was close enough to hear his musing. She was pretty, and he summoned up a smile for her.

"Just talking to myself," he told her. "They say that's a sign of an addled mind."

She grinned back at him. "I suppose that depends on what you're talking about."

"How old I'm getting. That's what I was talking about."

She gave him an intent look and said, "You don't look old to me. In fact, you look like you're in the prime of life."

Fury chuckled. "Thanks. I reckon that's what I needed to hear, whether it's true or not."

"Oh, it's true." Her blue eyes sparkled at him. She blushed a little, probably aware that she was flirting shamelessly with him, Fury thought. She went off to the kitchen before he could say anything else, but that was all right. He already felt better.

When he finished his meal, he left two bits on the table for her before he went to pay his bill to a big Dutchman at a counter just inside the door. When he stepped out onto the sidewalk, he paused, hooked his thumbs in his belt, and enjoyed the warmth of the morning sun for a minute before heading down to the livery stable to check on the dun and the mule.

There were tragedies aplenty in the world, thought Fury. People died needlessly every day, leaving even more pain and suffering behind them in the wake of their deaths. But life kept rolling along, too, and you could see that in the bright yellow rays of the sun and a pretty girl's smile. The only way to miss out on the misery was to give up on all the good times, too.

Fury wasn't ready to do that. Not by a long shot.

Two more days had gone by. Fury had spent most of that time playing poker in Fogle's Place, nursing a beer as he played, rather than wasting his money on the panther piss that Fogle brewed up in tubs behind the saloon. Most of the time, the game was low stakes, and the other players were cowboys and farmers from the surrounding area. That was fine with Fury. He was passing the time, nothing more. In two days of playing, he was about twenty dollars ahead of the game, and he was satisfied with that.

Maddie was still working the place, but after approaching him once, she left him alone. He'd been polite enough when he told her he wasn't interested, but he supposed she saw something in his eyes that warned her off. He was in a better mood now than when he had returned to Waco, but that was a fragile thing, easily shattered.

Billy and Judd had been in the saloon a couple of times, too, while he was there, but they didn't bother him, just had a couple of drinks and left. Tangling with him once was enough.

He was leaning back in his chair, a short, unlit stogie clenched between his teeth, studying the cards he held in his hand. Shit, king high. He'd keep the king and the ten, he had just decided, and throw away the rest. Couldn't get any worse.

Jase Sutton pushed past the batwings and came into the saloon.

Fury spotted Whitelaw's foreman, and the feeling inside him— not peace or contentment, exactly, but perhaps acceptance— evaporated instantly. Tossing his cards into the center of the table, Fury said, "I'm out."

The other players looked at him curiously but didn't say anything. Fury reached down, picked up his hat from the floor beside his chair, and stood up. Sutton was coming across the long, narrow room toward him.

Fury put his hat on, aware that most of the people in the saloon were watching him. Felicia Whitelaw's kidnapping and her brother's murder were still subjects for plenty of conversation in Waco, and folks knew he had been involved in the hunt for Felicia. As Sutton came to a stop in front of him, Fury asked quietly, "Has something happened?"

"I ain't sure," replied the old-timer. "All I know is Pres sent me to town to fetch you. He was hopin' you were still here and wouldn't mind ridin' out to the ranch."

"I'll get my horse," Fury said without hesitation.

Five minutes later, Fury and Sutton were riding along the river road. It was a cloudy afternoon, and the Brazos reflected that grayness. Might be some rain later, Fury thought.

"Those fellas Nash and Oakley come to the house earlier," Sutton said after they had ridden in silence for several minutes. "Said they wanted to talk to Pres. He went into his study with 'em, then came out a little later and told me to go and get you. I reckon it's got somethin' to do with Felicia."

That seemed likely to Fury, too, but he was puzzled by the connection of Nash and Oakley. They had stumbled on to the raid by accident and hadn't gone along on the search party. From what Fury had heard of them, they owned a small ranch that was only moderately successful. They did their best and got along somehow, like thousands of other settlers.

There was no point in wasting time and energy on speculation, Fury decided. He and Sutton would be at the ranch soon enough, and then he would find out what was going on.

He saw the horses belonging to Nash and Oakley tied to the porch rail in front of the house as he and Sutton reined in. Peyton and Frank Whitelaw were waiting on the porch, their faces tense. As Fury and Sutton climbed the steps, Peyton asked, "What's going on, Jase? Pa won't tell us a thing!"

"He sure looked excited when he got through talking to those two men," added Frank. "I'll bet it's something about Felicia!"

Fury agreed with the youngster. News of Felicia was probably the only thing that would have prompted Whitelaw to send for him.

"Now, boys, I don't know no more than you do," said Sutton. "I reckon we all got to be patient until your pa's talked to Mr. Fury here."

"Have *you* heard anything about Felicia, Mr. Fury?" asked Frank.

Fury shook his head. "I'm in the dark just like the rest of you."

He followed Sutton into the house. There was no sign of Muriel Whitelaw or Laurel, and Fury was grateful for that. Sutton went down the first-floor hallway and rapped his knobby knuckles against a door. Whitelaw's voice came from the other side. "Who is it?"

Sutton opened the door and said, "Got Mr. Fury here like you wanted, Pres."

Whitelaw appeared in the doorway and held out a hand to Fury. "Thank you for coming, Mr. Fury," he said. Although his face was still gray and haggard, as it had been the last time Fury had seen him, there was more life in his eyes.

Fury shook hands with him, then Whitelaw ushered him into the room. Bob Nash and Lester Oakley were sitting in wing chairs near a big rolltop desk. Whitelaw closed the door and waved Fury into another chair, then took a seat himself.

"You remember Mr. Nash and Mr. Oakley?"

Fury nodded to the men. "Howdy, gents." They had their hats in their laps and looked a little uncomfortable in these surroundings. Big dark bookshelves filled up most of the wall space. There were probably as many leather-bound volumes in this room as there were in the whole city of Waco, Fury thought.

Whitelaw put his walking stick across his knees and leaned forward in his chair. "Mr. Nash and Mr. Oakley have an idea about how to recover Felicia from those savages. I want you to hear this, Mr. Fury."

His eyes narrowed in surprise, Fury looked at the two men. He wouldn't have expected them to come up with a plan to rescue Felicia. They had been quick enough to pitch in and try to stop her abduction, but after that they had been more concerned with their own business than with helping out.

"Is that so?" Fury said coolly. "What's this idea of yours, boys?"

Lester Oakley licked his lips nervously and said, "Well, it's Bob's idea, really. I didn't come up with it. Fact is, I ain't too sure about it. But we're partners, so I reckon I'll do whatever Bob thinks is best."

Fury's gaze searched Nash's narrow face. He waited.

"Look," said Nash, "I don't want you to think me and Lester are yellow or anything."

"Nobody thinks that," Whitelaw spoke up, "not with the way you tried to help my daughter."

"No, sir, maybe not, but some folks might ask why we dragged our feet a little about comin' back to see you. It ain't that we were scared, so much as it was we were just waitin' to see what the Rangers came up with."

Fury was getting impatient, and Nash wasn't making a lot of sense. "What's this about?" he asked again.

"Well," said Nash, "it's like this. Lester and me, we've had a little experience at gettin' white folks back from the Indians. We rode into the hill country several times and brought back white captives with us."

"You're saying you rescued these people from Indians?" Fury asked tensely.

"Nope. We *bought* 'em back."

Fury's jaw tightened. He had heard of such things before. "Go on."

"Well, it's simple enough." Nash seemed to relax a bit as he warmed to his subject. "A Comanche's more interested in a good horse than he is a woman. When we were still livin' down south of here, we heard about some white women who'd been stolen in an Indian raid. We got together some horses and rode into the hills after 'em. When those Comanches saw what we had to trade, they gave us the women and took the horses."

"Scariest damn time I ever spent," Oakley put in fervently.

"Why didn't they just take the horses, keep the women, and kill the two of you?" asked Fury.

"Well, now, that's a good question," replied Nash. "I put it down to a redskin's natural love of tradin'. Oh, they could've killed us, all right. We knew it, and they knew it, too. But I reckon that wouldn't have been enough of a challenge for them. It was more fun for them to work a swap with us." Nash shrugged his shoulders. "All I know for sure is that we went after white prisoners that way three times, and we got back with them and our own hair all three times."

"You can check it out if you think we're lyin'," said Oakley. "Just write to the mayor down there in New Braunfels. He can tell you all about it."

"I'm not going to waste time doing that, not with Felicia being held prisoner by savages," said Whitelaw. To Fury, he went on, "I've heard their story twice now, and I believe it. What do you think?"

"Indians like to trade," Fury said slowly. "It's a sort of game to them, like nearly everything else. So I reckon these fellas could be telling the truth." He looked intently at Nash and Oakley. "Just what is it you intend to do?"

"Mr. Whitelaw here has got the finest horses in this part of the state," said Nash. "I figure if we take a good-sized string of them and head out, those Indians'll find us. When they do, we'll trade the horses to them for Miss Whitelaw."

"Might work," Fury admitted. "But why did you wait so long to suggest it?"

"Like I said, we were waitin' to see if you and the Rangers had any luck findin' her." Nash grimaced. "Besides, like Lester said, it's pretty damn scary to try to pull off something like this. If anything goes wrong, you wind up dead in a hurry. We talked it over for a long time before we decided we ought to come see Mr. Whitelaw."

"And you finally decided you ought to give it a try?"

"We're Texans," Nash declared. "We can't just sit by and let that gal be . . . let her stay a prisoner if we might be able to help get her back."

"I think it's a good idea," said Whitelaw. "By God, we've got to do *something*. This waiting is killing Muriel."

"We could be ready to ride first thing tomorrow morning," said Nash.

"There's one more thing," Whitelaw went on. "You men will be taking a big risk. My . . . my daughter's life is priceless to me. If you bring her back, I can promise that you'll be well paid."

Fury frowned. Whitelaw seemed determined to give money to everybody who crossed his path. Fury still felt a little guilty about taking the money Whitelaw had pressed on him.

But the rancher was right. Nash and Oakley would be risking their lives, much more so than Fury had been by riding with a troop of Rangers. They would be going into the wilderness alone, taking with them the most tempting target of all for renegade Comanches—horses. If they were going to take that chance, they deserved to be paid.

"Whatever you think is fair, Mr. Whitelaw," Nash said.

"I'll give you five hundred now," said Whitelaw, swinging around in his chair to open a drawer in the rolltop desk. "You'll need that to outfit yourselves. I'll furnish mounts if you want them, too, in addition to the horses you'll take to trade for Felicia."

"Our own horses'll do fine for ridin'," Nash told him.

"All right. And when you get back with my daughter, there'll be two thousand dollars more."

"That's plenty generous," Nash said with a nod. "Thank you kindly, Mr. Whitelaw."

"No, sir. Thank *you*."

Fury's hat was balanced on his knee. He picked it up, unsure why Whitelaw had sent Jase Sutton into town to bring him out here. "If you just wanted my opinion of this plan," he said to the rancher, "I think it's worth a try. If these gents have done such a thing before, it might work again."

Whitelaw looked at him in surprise. "You don't understand, Mr. Fury," he said. "I want more than your opinion. I want you to go with them."

CHAPTER
10
·····················

Fury blinked in surprise, and Nash and Oakley looked taken aback, too. "Why me?" Fury asked after several seconds of silence had gone by.

"I trust you, Mr. Fury." Quickly, he added to Nash and Oakley, "Not that I don't trust you two gentlemen, as well. But I've done some checking on you, Mr. Fury. You have quite a reputation as a frontiersman."

"That Ranger captain seemed to think my reputation made me the next thing to an outlaw," grunted Fury.

"Ben Sprague is a good man. But he sometimes sees things too much in black and white. I suppose that comes from being a lawman and dealing with criminals all the time."

"Could be," Fury said. "I don't know that these fellas want me along, though."

"Always glad for company," said Nash, although he didn't sound completely sincere to Fury. "In case we run into trouble, I'd be damn glad to have another gun along, in fact."

"Yeah," Oakley said sullenly. "You can come along."

"And my boys Peyton and Frank will ride with you as well," announced Whitelaw.

"Wait a minute," said Nash, looking more uneasy now. "We take too big a bunch out there, the Indians are liable not to deal with us."

"Peyton and Frank are the only other ones going," said Whitelaw. "Surely five of you won't be enough to scare off any Indians."

Whitelaw's declaration had surprised Fury as much as it did Nash and Oakley. The man had already lost a son and a daughter to the Indians; why was he sending out two more children into such a risky situation?

"Do Peyton and Frank know about this?" asked Fury.

Whitelaw shook his head. "Not all the details, no. But they've been badgering me for days now to take their guns and go looking for their sister. This will give them an opportunity to find her." He looked at Nash and Oakley. "Besides, while I trust you men, I'm not in the habit of turning over a string of horses to someone I don't know that well. I'll feel better about it if I've got some kin along."

Oakley looked vaguely resentful, but Nash just nodded and said, "I reckon we can understand that." His understanding sounded a little forced to Fury, though.

This development made up Fury's mind for him. If the Whitelaw boys were going along to keep an eye on their father's horses, then *he* was going along to keep an eye on *them*. He had a hunch that that was the real reason Preston Whitelaw wanted him along on this little expedition.

"I know you'll expect to be paid, too, Mr. Fury," began Whitelaw, but Fury waved off the words.

"We'll talk about that after we get back," he said.

"All right," nodded Whitelaw. "If the three of you will be here tomorrow morning, before first light, I'll have the horses ready for you, along with plenty of provisions."

Fury stood up. "I'll be ready to ride," he said.

As he left the room, he thought Nash and Oakley looked a little disappointed in the way things had worked out.

Peyton, Frank, and Sutton had been waiting outside the door of Whitelaw's study, and the rancher called them in as Fury went out. Nash and Oakley stayed behind, probably to explain the plan to the youngsters and the old foreman. Frustrated by their older brother's death and their sister's kidnapping, Peyton and Frank had been itching for some action.

Well, it looked like they were going to get it, Fury thought as he swung up on the dun and rode back toward Waco.

Whitelaw had promised to provide the supplies they would need for their journey, but that afternoon Fury bought plenty of powder and shot for the Dragoon and cartridges for the Sharps. The clerk in the general store grinned across the counter at him and asked, "Goin' huntin'?"

"Reckon you could say that," Fury replied honestly.

He had no reason to distrust Nash and Oakley. On the contrary, they were going out of their way to try to help the Whitelaw family, just as they had done when they confronted the Indians. At the same time, he figured they had hoped to be well paid when they came to Whitelaw with their offer of assistance. It was possible that they had been lying, that they intended to run off with the horses Whitelaw would provide to ransom his daughter from the Comanches. If that was what they had in mind, the addition of Fury, Peyton, and Frank to the party had scotched that plan.

Likely everything was on the up and up. Even if it was, Fury didn't want to take a chance on running short of ammunition.

He paid one more visit to Fogle's Place that night, but stayed only long enough to drink two beers. He wanted a clear head in the morning. Now that he had a purpose again, he slept surprisingly well, too, and woke up in plenty of time to be riding along the Brazos road well before daylight.

The Whitelaw house was brightly lit when he got there. Lamps shone in nearly every window, and men carried lanterns in the barn and the corrals. Horses neighed and shuffled while cowboys called out to each other. The place was a beehive of activity.

Nash and Oakley sat on their horses in front of the house. Preston Whitelaw stood on the porch, his arm around his wife. Muriel Whitelaw wore a dressing gown, and her hair was loose. She still looked pale and drawn, but at least there was some animation in her eyes again.

"You'll find her," she was saying to Nash and Oakley as Fury rode up. "I know you'll find her."

"Yes, ma'am, I surely do hope so," replied Nash with a nod of his head.

"We'll do our best," promised Oakley.

Whitelaw raised his free hand in greeting to Fury. "Good morning," he called. "Are you ready to ride?"

Fury nodded. "Ready as I'll ever be."

Whitelaw gestured toward a pack mule. Nash was holding the animal's reins. "You should have plenty of supplies there," said Whitelaw. "There's food, ammunition, bandages and medical gear."

"We ain't goin' to war, Mr. Whitelaw," Oakley pointed out.

"I hope not, but I'd rather you be prepared and not need any of those things."

Fury could go along with that thinking. He had enough supplies in his saddlebags so that he could get along for several days by himself if he needed to.

"Jase is getting the horses ready for you," Whitelaw went on. "And Peyton and Frank should be ready to go soon, too."

As if the young men had been waiting for his comment, they emerged from the house. Instead of the work shirts and pants Fury had seen them in on all his other visits, they were wearing range clothes now, and each of them had a gunbelt strapped around his waist. Peyton carried a Sharps slanting breech carbine almost identical to Fury's, and Frank had a breech-loading single-shot Jennings rifle.

"We're here, Pa," Peyton said.

Whitelaw nodded. "Jase'll bring your horses around in a minute. Say goodbye to your mother, boys."

Muriel embraced both of them, and the air of optimism she had displayed a few minutes earlier was shaken a little. Her eyes glistened with tears as she said farewell to her remaining sons. "Be careful," she told them. "Please be careful."

Both of the boys looked embarrassed. "You know we will, Ma," Frank said. "Don't worry none about us. We'll be fine, and when we get back, we'll have Felicia with us."

"I know," said Muriel. "I know you will."

A few minutes later, Jase Sutton and several of the Whitelaw ranch hands rode up to the house from the barn and the corrals. They brought with them twenty unsaddled horses, along with the two mounts for Peyton and Frank. In the lanternlight, Fury studied the horses, and he had to admit they were fine-looking animals. A Comanche chief would probably drool at the prospect of owning them. To an Indian, twenty horses like this would be worth a hell of a lot more than one white woman, no matter how young and beautiful she was.

"Here they are, Pres," Sutton said to Whitelaw. "The best o' the herd."

"Thanks, Jase."

"Sure you don't want me to go along, too?"

Whitelaw smiled at his long-time foreman. "I'd like that, but I need you here. I'm still not getting around well enough to keep the ranch running. I wish this damned foot would go ahead and heal up."

Peyton and Frank stepped down from the porch and took the reins of their horses from Sutton. They mounted up. Frank looked over at Fury and nodded. "Good morning, sir."

"Morning," Fury returned the greeting.

"Jase told us about some of the things you've done, Mr. Fury," Peyton said. "Scouting with Kit Carson, leading wagon trains, fighting Indians and outlaws, trapping in the Rockies . . . It's an honor to ride with you, sir."

"Let's just hope it works out, boys," Fury said briskly. It was too early in the morning for a recitation of his supposed accomplishments.

"Ready to ride, Fury?" asked Nash.

"Whenever you are."

Nash nodded and swung his horse around. Oakley followed suit. Fury was about to do likewise when a sudden pounding of hooves sounded from the direction of the corrals.

"Wait up!" called a young female voice. "Wait for me!"

While Fury and the others stared in surprise, Laurel Whitelaw came racing around the house on horseback, riding a sleek bay mare. She was wearing boots, denim pants, and a red-checked shirt that must have belonged to one of her brothers. Her long blonde hair was tucked up under a shapeless felt hat to keep it out of the way. She reined in, coming to a stop alongside Peyton.

Her father was the first one to find his voice. He thundered, "Young lady, just what in blue blazes do you think you're doing?"

"I'm going to help get Felicia back," Laurel replied calmly.

"Laurel, no!" cried her mother.

Fury's back had stiffened. He looked at Preston Whitelaw. Either the rancher would put a stop to this ridiculous notion, or Fury would have to. There was no possible way Laurel could go with them.

"Take that horse back to the barn and unsaddle him, Laurel," Whitelaw said wearily. "You know you can't go."

"Why not?" demanded Laurel, her voice becoming angry. "Pate and Frank are going. Felicia's my sister, too, and I've got a right to help!"

"Peyton and Frank are young men," said Whitelaw, with the air of a man talking to a headstrong child, a man who often had to explain things that should have been obvious. "I asked them to go. I'm asking you to stop this foolishness."

"It's not foolishness!" exclaimed Laurel. "Pa, I think I'm going to go crazy if I have to sit around here much longer the way things have been. I've got to get out and *do* something."

"Ridin' into Comanche country ain't a very good idea, miss," Nash pointed out.

"You're going to do it," Laurel said sharply, swinging around in the saddle to face him.

"Lester and me are bein' well paid by your pa to take that chance, too," replied Nash.

Laurel turned her attention to Fury. "What about you, Mr. Fury? Is my father paying you, too?"

"He is," Fury answered honestly. "That's not the only reason I'm going, though. I want to see your sister safely back home."

"But that's what *I* want, too!"

"Problem is," Fury said quietly, "having you along with us would make that a lot harder, Miss Whitelaw. We'd be watching out for you instead of concentrating on finding Felicia and getting her back from the Indians."

Laurel tossed her head, and a few strands of the fine blonde hair slipped out from under the old hat. "Nobody has to watch out for me. I can take care of myself."

"On the frontier, miles from home, surrounded by Indians?" Fury shook his head. "I'm sorry."

Laurel glared at him, then looked at her parents again. "Mama, you understand, don't you?" she pleaded.

"I understand that I want you to get down off that horse, march into this house, and put your regular clothes back on," Muriel said firmly. "I swear, I never thought I'd see a daughter of mine dressed like a cowboy!"

"Well . . . well . . ." Laurel looked around and saw opposition on every face, from her parents and her brothers to Fury, Nash, and Oakley. Even old Jase Sutton, whose special pet she had been ever since she was a baby, was frowning at her. "Well, hell!" she exploded.

She yanked the mare around and spurred it into motion, racing around the house and past the barn. Whitelaw watched her go and then sighed. "She'll have to ride off her anger and disappointment, but she'll get over it. I'm sorry for the delay, gentlemen." He came down off the porch, leaning heavily on his cane, and shook hands with Fury, Nash, and Oakley before he got to his sons. He clasped their hands a little longer in farewell, then stepped back and lifted the walking stick in a salute. "Godspeed and good luck!"

The five riders turned. Hazing the horses ahead of them, they rode away from the ranch. The hooves kicked up dust on the river road, pale gray in the faint pre-dawn light.

CHAPTER
11

· ·

"Know much about Comanches?" asked Bob Nash as he rode beside Fury.

"Traded shots with some of them up in Kansas a few years back," replied Fury. "That's the last time I ran into any of them, though."

"They get around, all right. A Comanche would rather be movin' than stayin' in one place, no matter how nice it is. That's why they prize horses so much. I wish Lester and me had got a better look at the ones who ran off with Miss Whitelaw. Then we'd know for sure we're dealin' with Comanches."

"Could've been Kiowa, I reckon," put in Oakley. "Them Kiowa are known as far-ranging raiders. But then they might've even been some Cheyenne. Don't generally find them south of the Red River."

Now that they had left the ranch, both Nash and Oakley seemed a little friendlier. Nash said to Fury, "I was just askin' in case you had any ideas which way we should head out."

"That trail I followed led southwest."

"Yeah, but the Brazos runs northwest," Nash said dubiously. "The Indians like that river. I've heard that somewhere up around the headwaters, they got themselves a damn big village. Comancheria, they call it, though some folks will use that name for all of western Texas. Can't really blame 'em, either. Most of it's still Comanche land."

"So you think the Indians who took Felicia just headed southwest to throw off anybody who might try to follow them?"

Nash nodded in response to Fury's question. "Yep, that's what I think, all right. I think when we come to the ford up here a ways, we ought to cross over and follow the north bank of the Brazos, clear to the Seven Fingers country if we have to."

Peyton Whitelaw spoke up. "But what if you're wrong, Mr. Nash?"

Fury had been thinking the same thing.

"Well, maybe we won't follow the Brazos all the way up. If we don't run into the Indians we're lookin' for, we can always cross the river again and swing over toward the Colorado. First thing I want to do, though, since we're headin' north to start out, is stop by my ranch for a few minutes. I forgot to give my woman that money your daddy paid us, and I sure as hell don't want to carry it off with me into the wilderness. Wouldn't do my woman no good if I took it with me and never came back."

Nash had just assumed that his decision to head north and then west wouldn't be challenged. But if this expedition had a leader, Fury supposed it was Bob Nash. Nash and Oakley were the only ones with any experience at this sort of thing, and Oakley was obviously more dull-witted than his partner, following Nash's lead most of the time.

As the sun was coming up, they reached a place where the river was shallow enough to swim the horses across. The animals balked at first, but with some yelling and slapping with the ropes they carried, Fury and the others were able to drive them to the other side of the Brazos. They emerged shaking water from their sleek hides.

The warmth of the day increased rapidly once the sun was up, drying the wet clothes of the riders. In fact, Fury thought, the day was turning unseasonably warm, more like summer than spring. He slipped a piece of jerky from his saddlebags and began to chew it. Breakfast had come mighty early this morning, and it would be a long time until they stopped for a midday meal.

As worried as Peyton and Frank were about Felicia, they still took advantage of the opportunity to ask Fury a lot of questions about the things he had seen and done during his years of drifting along the frontier. He answered them as best he could, feeling slightly uncomfortable because the young men obviously regarded him as some sort of hero. Fury had never seen himself in that light. He was just a man who had given in to his natural wanderlust, and it had gotten him into trouble more than once. There was nothing glamorous about it.

He kept up the conversation with the Whitelaw brothers, anyway. Talking would help distract them from the danger they might be riding into. Brooding and getting nervous wouldn't help matters.

Around mid-morning, the group approached a small ranch house. It was built of logs, constructed in the dogtrot style which was so common down here that some people even called it a "Texas cabin." There was a barn out back of the house, along with a small vegetable garden. Fury saw a herd of cattle grazing in a hilly pasture nearby.

"That's our spread," Nash said without any particular pride in his voice.

Fury could understand why. The cabin was in poor repair, and the barn looked like it had been thrown together haphazardly, with no thought of permanence. The cattle, from what he could see of them, seemed to be second-rate animals, rangy and half-wild. A crop had been planted in the garden in meandering rows that never ran straight for more than a few inches.

There were little farms and cow outfits like this all along the Texas frontier. This was good land, land that would easily support a man and his family if he was willing to work. Most of the settlers were more than willing—but some weren't. Nash and Oakley seemed to be that kind, judging from the appearance of their ranch. They would work when they had to, but they would probably never take the time and trouble to make this place into a paying proposition.

With the five-hundred dollars they had already been paid and the two thousand more that had been promised by Whitelaw if they brought Felicia back safe and sound, they could afford to leave this ranch, go somewhere else, and make a new start. Or they could take the money and go on a spree that might last for weeks or even months. Even less likely was the possibility that they might put the profits of this perilous trip back into the spread and try to improve it. *If* they came back alive, of course.

Whichever course they followed, it would be none of his business, Fury told himself. His only concern now was that they make this stop a short one, so that they could get on about their business.

A woman stood in the dogtrot between the two sections of the log house. She was working a churn, but she stopped when she spotted the riders coming, pushing the string of horses ahead of them. She hurried out to meet them.

Her long hair, dark as midnight, was braided and hung on the shoulders of her buckskin dress. Her flat, bronze face was impassive as she watched the men ride up. Fury figured she was a Comanche, which came as a surprise since he hadn't thought of Nash as a squaw man. But that would explain how Nash had come to know so much about the Comanche and their ways.

Nash swung down from his saddle and took a small leather pouch from the pocket of his buckskin jacket. "Here," he said, handing the pouch to the woman. "Almost forgot this."

She took the pouch but didn't open it to look at the money inside. Instead she stared up into Nash's face and said, "You are still going to do this thing?"

"Got to. I took Mr. Whitelaw's money and gave him my word." Nash glanced over his shoulder at Fury and grinned uncomfortably. "My wife don't think it's such a good idea, goin' out to look for them Comanches. They're her people, you know."

The woman said, "This is why I know that someday they will kill you."

"Not me, sugar," Nash assured her. Fury knew he sounded more confident than he felt. Nash, just like Oakley, was obviously nervous about what they were about to do.

The Indian woman stood there stiffly as Nash took her gently into his arms and kissed her. She made no reply as he told her goodbye and mounted up again. Her face was stony.

Nash waved to her and led the group away from the ranch, heading back toward the Brazos. When they were out of earshot, he said sheepishly, "She ain't as contrary as she seemed back there. She just don't like it when Lester and me take chances. And no matter how you look at it, we'll be runnin' a risk out there."

Oakley added, "I reckon she'll perk up a mite when we get back with Miss Whitelaw and collect the rest o' that money."

Fury didn't say anything. It was none of his business how Nash got along with his wife—or didn't get along. His job now was to keep Peyton and Frank Whitelaw alive and to bring back their sister Felicia safe and sound.

When they reached the river again, they turned sharply northwest to follow its course. The landscape here was the same sort of gently rolling hills as was found around

Waco. As they left the settlement farther and farther behind, the woods became thicker because fewer fields had been cleared for cultivation. For a time that first day, they saw an occasional farmhouse, but those became fewer and farther between. By nightfall, they were in country that had never known a plow or the hooves of domestic cattle.

When Nash had selected a campsite, Peyton and Frank dismounted and got to work hobbling the horses that would serve as Felicia's ransom if all went as planned. There was no other way to keep the animals from straying at night. Lester Oakley gathered some wood for a fire, and they had a leaping blaze going as the sun went down and night closed in around them.

"We'll build a good-sized fire every night," commented Nash. "That's one more thing to draw those Indians to us."

Someone was bound to notice them sooner or later, all right, thought Fury. He just hoped it was the *right* Indians who did.

Fury, Nash, and Oakley took turns standing watch that night, letting Peyton and Frank sleep through. Once the two young men had been out here for a while and had proven themselves more, they could take over part of that responsibility. For the time being, however, Nash didn't want to take a chance on one of the boys dozing off while he was on duty, and Fury had to agree with that thinking.

All during Fury's shift, he was uneasy, as if he was being watched. That was possible, he supposed; the Indians could have already found them and might be keeping an eye on the camp until they were good and ready to confront the white men. All Fury knew for sure was that the night passed quietly, with no trouble.

Early the next morning, they were on the move again.

This was pretty country, Fury thought as they rode along the valley of the Brazos. Game was abundant. He saw deer, foxes, bobcats, raccoons, possums, armadilloes, once even a band of gray wolves in the distance. Mustang grapes grew on vines that snaked through the branches of the oaks, and there were wild plum trees blossoming. The temperature was unusually warm again, warm enough so that Fury began to have a few misgivings. When it got too hot at this time of year, that was sometimes a warning that a late cold snap was on the way, and those blue northers could be brutal. That would be an added complication the searchers didn't need.

For the time being, though, there was nothing to do but ride along and enjoy the scenery.

Fury had to give Peyton and Frank credit. They hadn't complained once, even though they were obviously not used to being in the saddle this much. Pate, as the older brother had asked Fury to call him, even downed a good-sized buck with one shot from his Sharps late that afternoon, and thanks to him they had fresh meat for supper. Nash built a big fire once again, and the smell of the venison sizzling over the flames floated deliciously along the riverbank.

Not sitting too close to the fire because of the heat it gave off, Fury watched the sun set behind the hills and bluffs to the west. He didn't know how long Nash intended to follow the Brazos before crossing it again and heading toward the Colorado River. They had already covered a lot of ground, but there was still a lot of west Texas in front of them.

Pate and Frank wandered over and sat down next to Fury. "How far do you reckon we've come, Mr. Fury?" Frank asked.

Fury considered. The terrain had been fairly easy to cross, and they had made good time. "Close to forty miles, I'd say," he replied.

"We've never been this far west before," said Pate. "We used to talk about coming out here when we got older. Joshua wanted a place of his own. We figured we'd start a new ranch out here."

Pate's voice was wistful, and it caught a little, showing the grief over his brother's death he was still feeling. That pain would ease with time, Fury knew, but time was about the only thing that would help it.

After everyone had eaten, the brothers turned in, rolling in their blankets against what was likely to be a cool night, despite the heat of the day. Nash and Oakley brought out a tattered, creased deck of cards and invited Fury to play a few hands of poker with them, but Fury shook his head. He leaned back against his saddle, which was sitting on the ground behind him, tipped his hat down over his eyes, and dozed off. His turn at standing watch would not come until later.

He wasn't sure how long he slept, but he came awake abruptly. Pate and Frank were both still asleep nearby, and Fury spotted Lester Oakley on the other side of the fire, rolled in his own blankets and snoring loud enough to wake the dead.

Something had disturbed Fury, but what was it? Where was Bob Nash?

A slight movement in some nearby trees caught Fury's eye. It was little more than a faint shifting of shadows, but that was enough to alert him that something was happening. Keeping his eyes slitted so that anybody watching might not notice that he was awake, he began edging his hand toward the butt of his gun.

Suddenly, there was a noise from the woods, a quick scuffling and then a sharp cry. A shape plunged out of the thick shadows beneath the trees, stumbled and went down. The fire had burned down quite a bit, but it still gave off enough light for Fury to recognize the figure as human. As he surged to his feet and drew his gun, another person leaped out of the woods and jumped on the first one. Fury recognized the newcomer as Bob Nash.

Nash's gun was in his hand, and as he came down hard with his knees on the midsection of the other man, he jammed the barrel of the weapon against his opponent's neck. "Got you now, you sneakin'—"

Nash stopped short, seeing the same thing that Fury now saw to his amazement. The intruder's hat had fallen off when he fell, and long blonde hair spilled out of it. The man Nash had jumped wasn't a man at all.

"Please, please don't kill me," begged Laurel Whitelaw.

CHAPTER
12
· · · · · · · · · · · · · · · · · · · ·

Nash recoiled as if he'd suddenly found himself squatting on a rattlesnake. "What the hell!" he exclaimed.

Pate, Frank, and Oakley jerked up out of their blankets, their sleep disturbed by the commotion. "Laurel!" cried Pate. "What are you doing here?" Frank and Oakley were equally flabbergasted.

The only one who seemed calm was Fury, and that was because he kept a tight rein on his own surprise. He strode over to Laurel, who had sat up and was gasping for the breath Nash had knocked out of her when he jumped on her. Kneeling beside her, the Colt still in his hand, Fury asked, "Anybody chasing you?"

Laurel shook her head without saying anything. She was still too busy dragging air into her lungs.

Fury slid his gun back into its holster. If the girl was alone, she was no threat.

He stood up, stared down at her for a moment, then extended a hand. She took it after a second's hesitation, and he hauled her to her feet. "I'd ask you what the hell you're doing here, miss," Fury said, "but I reckon I already know."

The memory of the scene Laurel had made when the rescue party left the Whitelaw ranch two mornings earlier was clear in Fury's mind. Obviously, Laurel *hadn't* gotten over her anger at being left out, as her father had said she would.

"I've come to help," said Laurel, trying to make her voice firm but revealing by a slight quiver how shaken she was. "You didn't have any right to leave me behind and take Pate and Frank. Felicia's my sister, too."

"So you told us," Fury said dryly.

"Miss, you came mighty near bein' killed a couple of minutes ago," said Nash. He had holstered his gun, too. "When I heard somebody skulkin' around out there in the woods, I figured the

Comanches had come to spy on us." He looked at Fury and went on, "I snuck out to take a look, saw there was just one man and that he wasn't an Indian. Figured he was up to no good, so I jumped him. Turned out it wasn't even a man."

"I'm sorry if you're disappointed," Laurel said acidly.

"No use wrangling about it now," said Fury. "We've got to decide what we're going to do with her."

Pate said, "She can't come with us, that's for sure. She's just a kid."

"I am not! I'm a full-growed woman!" protested Laurel.

That wasn't quite the case, Fury thought. Laurel still had some growing up to do. But as he looked at the way her breasts filled out that borrowed shirt she wore and the fullness of her hips in those tight denim pants, he knew one thing—she was old enough to cause trouble.

"We can't turn around and take her back," Fury said. "We're two full days out of Waco, and we can't afford the time. However, one of you boys could ride with her and make sure she gets back safe."

Pate and Frank both shook their heads. "No, sir," said Frank. "We're in this, and we aim to stay in it to the end."

Fury glanced at Nash and Oakley and dismissed the thought before it was even fully formed. Nash was nominally in charge here and couldn't turn back. And Fury wouldn't trust Oakley to spend two days on the trail alone with the girl. Not the way Oakley's gaze had fastened on Laurel's heaving bosom as she tried to catch her breath.

To tell the truth, he wasn't comfortable with the idea of any of them turning around and going back. Pate and Frank had turned out to be good companions, and he had a feeling they would make reliable allies if there was trouble. *He* couldn't leave, not after the promise he had made to Preston Whitelaw.

That left them no option. Laurel would have to go with them.

"Looks like there's six of us now," Fury said.

The other four men stared at him. Nash was the one who finally spoke. "We're takin' her with us?"

"I don't see that we've got any choice. None of us are willing to take her back, and she can't go back by herself."

"The little fool followed us out here by herself," Frank said peevishly. "I don't see why she can't go back the same way." Even as he spoke, though, it was obvious he was just letting out some of his anger and didn't mean what he said.

"Sit down," Fury told Laurel. "I think there's still some coffee left in the pot. Want some?"

She smiled weakly as she sank to the ground near the faintly flickering campfire. "I sure do," she said. "It gets cold out here at night."

She had probably never spent a night in the open before, thought Fury. She hadn't known what to expect when she began following them. But she had come on anyway, stubbornly daring—or maybe daringly stubborn would be more appropriate, Fury mused with a shadow of a grin.

"I still think we're making a mistake," groused Pate, but he and Frank rolled themselves up in their blankets again, as did Lester Oakley. Nash squatted on his haunches on the other side of the fire as Fury got a tin cup from their gear and filled it with coffee from the pot that had been sitting in the embers at the edge of the fire. Laurel took it from him and sipped gratefully at the still-hot brew.

"Where's your horse?" Fury asked her.

She inclined her head toward the trees. "Tied up out there in the woods, about a hundred yards away from here. I didn't want to ride too close. I was afraid you might hear me, or that the other horses would smell mine and start kicking up a ruckus."

"You have any food?"

"Some. I sneaked into the cookshack and picked up a few things before I rode out after you the other day."

Fury shook his head. "Your ma and pa must be worried sick about you."

"Well . . . I'm sorry about that." Laurel sounded like she really was. "I hated to cause them any more trouble, but I know I can help you get Felicia back."

Fury didn't see how Laurel could be of any assistance to them, but he supposed in her mind she was convinced of what she was saying. "I'll go out there and get your horse in a few minutes. It needs to be brought in with the others."

"Mr. Fury . . ." She laid a hand on his arm. "You're not really too angry with me, are you?"

"I wouldn't ask your brothers that question if I was you," he told her, avoiding the issue himself.

Laurel just smiled a little and drank her coffee. Fury asked her if she'd had supper, and she said that she had. He stood up and moved toward the trees, saying, "I'll bring your horse in." Not surprisingly, Bob Nash got to his feet as well and fell in step beside him.

Nash didn't say anything until they were out of earshot of the camp, making their way carefully through the shadows under the trees. Then, in a quiet voice, he declared, "That girl's goin' to be nothin' but trouble."

"Maybe not," said Fury. "You think your partner can keep his hands off her?"

Nash chuckled, even though Fury didn't see anything humorous about the question. "Ol' Lester's always had an eye for a pretty girl, all right." Nash's voice grew harder. "He'll do what I tell him to do, so don't worry about him."

"Then tell him to leave Laurel alone."

"I intend to," said Nash.

They found Laurel's horse without any trouble, its reins tied to a small juniper tree. Fury led it back to camp, unsaddled it, and rubbed it down despite Laurel's protest that she could take care of her own mount. When he was done, he went back to the fire and sat down beside her again.

"If you go on with us, you've got to give me your word that you'll do as you're told," he said. "If we give you an order, you obey it instantly, understand?"

"Sure."

"I mean it, Laurel. This isn't a church social out here. We have to be ready for trouble all the time. I'm not trying to frighten you, but if you don't follow orders, you could wind up getting all of us killed."

Even in the ruddy glow of the fire, her face was a little pale. "I understand," she said softly.

"You'd damned well better," Fury said curtly. Then, making his voice a bit more gentle, he went on, "And you'd better get some sleep. We've got another long day of riding in front of us tomorrow."

They had more than that facing them.

There was a strong south wind blowing when they got up, bringing with it more heat. By mid-morning everyone had shucked their jackets, and by noon, the men had rolled up the sleeves of their shirts and Laurel had followed suit. The downy golden hair on her forearms, combined with the honey-colored skin, was enough to make a man swallow hard if he looked at it too long.

Fury didn't like the heat. It was unnatural, and when it broke—as it was bound to do—they might be in for trouble. He kept an eye on the sky all afternoon, and when he spotted a line of low blue clouds that looked almost like distant mountains on the horizon, he reined in and pointed them out to the others.

"Take a look at that."

Laurel, Pate, and Frank didn't know what they were seeing, but Nash and Oakley did. Nash let out a low whistle and said, "I've been afraid of somethin' like that. It's been too warm."

"I don't understand," said Laurel. "What is it?"

Fury looked over at her and said, "Blue norther."

Her eyes widened. She and her brothers might not have lived in Texas long enough to recognize all the signs of an impending weather change, but she had heard that term before, used by old-timers with the awe and respect it deserved. Pate and Frank knew what Fury was talking about, too.

"You mean it's going to storm?" Laurel asked.

"That depends," said Fury with a shrug. "A norther doesn't always bring sleet or snow with it. Sometimes they're just dry and cold." He glanced up at the sky, which was almost cloudless. "Most of the time it's worse if it *is* dry. If there's snow, the clouds hold some of the warmth near the ground, keep the temperature from getting quite as cold. If it stays clear like this, though—"

"It'll get cold enough to freeze the *cojones* off a marble statue," Oakley finished for him, betraying more culture than Fury would have suspected. If he'd had to guess, he would have said that Oakley had never even seen a marble statue.

Pate and Frank grinned, Laurel blushed, and Nash gave his partner a stern glance. "Watch your language, Lester," he said. "There's a lady present, in case you forgot."

"I ain't forgot," said Oakley. He tried to smile at Laurel, but it came out more of a leer.

"Why don't we move along and cover as much ground as we can before the wind shifts around?" suggested Fury.

"Good idea," agreed Nash. The horse herd had stopped to graze, so he and Oakley got them moving again, trotting along the plains that ran beside the river. Pate and Frank took the flanks, as they usually did, leaving Fury and Laurel to bring up the rear.

"You still think I shouldn't have come, don't you?" she asked him.

"I *know* you shouldn't have come."

"But I haven't been any trouble. You haven't heard one complaint out of me so far."

"That's true enough," admitted Fury. "We haven't been riding together very long, though."

Laurel pressed her lips together in anger and looked straight ahead, pretending he wasn't there. That was all right with Fury.

They pushed on at a rapid clip. Fury felt the south wind die away, and the air became still and heavy. The line of blue clouds was closer now.

About a quarter of a mile ahead of them, a wooded bluff rose beside the river. Fury was watching the limbs of those oaks, some of which were covered with new leaves, when suddenly they whipped back and forth for a moment and then laid over toward the approaching riders.

"Get your coats on and hang on to your hats!" called Fury.

The warning was barely in time. Cold wind struck him in the face like a fist. He tugged his hat down tighter and leaned his head into the wind, then finished buttoning up his coat. Beside him, Laurel gasped at the sudden change.

The horses reacted as well, flinching back from the wind and trying to turn and go the other direction. It took the combined efforts of everyone to keep the animals bunched up and heading northwest. Nash pointed to the bluff where Fury had seen the first evidence of the norther's arrival and shouted, "Might be able to find a place out of the wind over there!"

Fury nodded in agreement and waved him on.

He had been at sea during some gales that made even the old sailors blanch, and he doubted now that those winds had been any stronger than these. In addition, the temperature was plummeting by the minute. It was almost enough to freeze a man's blood in his veins.

The mass of cold air must have been building for days, far up there across the Canadian border. When it finally got too large, it had spilled across the Rockies and rolled straight down the plains in the center of the country with nothing to stop it. The situation had taken a long time to develop, and Fury feared the cold weather would be with them for a while now that it was here.

Nash led the way into the lee of the bluff while the others drove the snorting, protesting horses behind him. The wind still blew here, but not as strongly as it did out in the open. Fury swung the dun around the horse herd and peered along the base of the bluff, searching for some sort of shelter. A cave would have been ideal, but there didn't appear to be one. The next best thing, he decided, was a jumble of large rocks about a hundred yards away. He rode to them, looked the place over, then signaled for the rest of the party to join him.

The boulders were big enough that they blocked the wind even more, and one of them, a massive, squarish block of stone, had enough of an overhang to provide some protection. They could build a fire there and keep from freezing to death. Luckily, there was plenty of wood in the area. Fuel for the blaze wouldn't be a problem.

As Pate, Frank, and Oakley began hobbling the horses, Fury and Laurel gathered wood. Laurel still hadn't complained any, but Fury knew she must be hurting from the norther's abrupt arrival. The cold was a chilling, bone-numbing thing that was all the more painful because less than an hour earlier, they had been sweating from the hot southerly breezes.

"I hate this!" Laurel finally burst out as she and Fury were piling up the wood underneath the overhang of the rock.

"Don't blame you," said Fury, his breath fogging thickly in front of his face as he spoke.

"No, you don't understand!" The wind was wailing and whining, even though its force was not strong here, and Laurel had to lift her voice to be heard over it. "I'm worried about Felicia! I hope she's somewhere warm!"

If Felicia was still alive, she was probably in a Comanche tepee, no doubt warmer and more sheltered from the elements than they were. Even if that was the case, however, Fury wouldn't have traded places with her.

"I'm sure she's fine," he told Laurel. "The Comanches aren't any more interested in freezing than we are."

Laurel glanced up at the sky. The thin blue clouds had arrived not long after the onslaught of the wind, but there were gaps in them revealing the lighter blue sky above. "What will we do if it snows?"

Fury knew as much about the weather as anybody who had spent much of his life outdoors. He checked the clouds, saw they didn't have the low, ominous, gray appearance of snow clouds, and shook his head. "It's not going to snow," he declared with relative certainty. "But it is going to be cold, awful cold."

For an instant, a smile played around Laurel's lips. "Cold enough to freeze the—"

"Let's just get the fire started, and maybe nothing will freeze off," Fury told her.

CHAPTER
13

·····················

For three nights and two days, the search party crouched there among those big rocks, trying to keep from freezing to death.

As Fury had predicted, there was no snow or sleet. In fact, by midnight of the first night, the clouds that had blown in with the norther were gone, leaving the sky clear and glittering with brilliant stars. The temperature dropped even more with darkness, plunging well below freezing.

Fury had found a small trickle of water, almost too tiny to be called a creek, about a hundred yards from the rocks where he and the others were camped. By the next morning, when he went to check the stream, there was a crust of ice over the top of it. The ice was thin and easily broken, but that was one more indication—as if they'd needed one—of how cold it was.

Luckily, there was plenty of wood around, so they were able to keep the fire burning brightly all night. They stood watch by twos, one person to keep an eye out for trouble, the other to feed the fire. Rolled tightly in their blankets, the sleepers were not too cold; the heat from the flames radiated against the overhang of rock and spread out over the camp. It wasn't as cozy as a nice snug log cabin, but considering how bad things could have been, Fury figured they were pretty lucky to have found this place.

Nash suggested they might be able to move on the next day, but the temperature was still below freezing. "We could ride in this weather, sure," Fury responded. "But the Indians won't be moving around. They'll be holed up somewhere until this cold snap breaks. We won't be able to come any closer to finding them by pushing on, so we'd just be taking a chance for nothing."

Unable to argue with Fury's logic, Nash just nodded in sullen agreement. The delay chafed at all of them, especially Laurel, but the best thing to do was simply wait until the cold weather eased its brutal grip.

For a while that first day, Pate and Frank tried to keep up a conversation, asking questions of Fury, but he wasn't in the mood to respond with much more than grunts. Finally the young men gave up. Laurel was already brooding, and Nash and Oakley were sunk in thoughts of their own. The camp was silent for the most part after that. The searchers just tried to keep warm and put all other concerns aside.

The second night was even colder than the first, and Fury felt the chill sinking into his bones. He moved stiffly when he got up the next morning. This time, when he went to fetch water, it was more difficult to chip through the ice with his Bowie knife. The creek wasn't going to freeze solid, not with the constant motion of the water underneath the layer of ice, but if this kept up he was going to be able to walk on it, Fury thought.

The sunshine was thin and weak and didn't bring much warmth with it, but along toward the middle of the second miserable afternoon, the wind finally died down. It had been howling for forty-eight hours now, and that was enough to drive a man crazy. The silence was a welcome relief as the wind's whine faded.

The worst of it was over, decided Fury. Sometime relatively soon, the wind would turn back around to the south, and when it did, warmth would return.

Nash agreed. "We'll be able to ride tomorrow," he commented that evening as the group made its supper on the usual beans, bacon, and biscuits.

"More than likely," said Fury with a nod.

"I'll be glad," said Laurel. "I hate to think about Felicia having to spend all this extra time with those savages."

"Don't you worry 'bout your sister," Oakley told her. "I reckon them Injuns made sure she stayed warm." The words could have been meant to comfort Laurel, but even though Oakley kept his face carefully expressionless, all of them heard the double meaning in his statement.

Fury's jaw tightened. He didn't like Oakley, and the more time he spent with the man, the greater that feeling grew. As for Nash, Fury couldn't pin him down. He seemed friendly enough most of the time, but there was something about him that made Fury unwilling to trust him completely. He would be glad when this job was over, one way or the other, so he wouldn't have to ride with the two men any more.

"We'll get an early start," Nash said into the awkward silence that followed Oakley's comment. "After another day or two, if we haven't run across any sign of the Indians we're lookin' for, we'll cut over toward the Colorado."

Fury approved of that strategy. Of course, the whole thing was hit or miss to a certain extent. They could ride within a mile of the band of Comanches holding Felicia and not know they were there. And Texas was a mighty big place. A man could look around out here for years and still maybe not find whatever it was he sought.

The prospect of doing something again lightened the mood of the camp. Pate and Frank became more talkative, and even Laurel brightened up a bit. By the time everybody was ready to turn in, they were anxious for morning to arrive, so that they could be on the move.

Fury had the first watch, along with Frank Whitelaw. It was Frank's job to keep the fire burning brightly, and he did it without complaint, occasionally talking to Fury in a low voice so that he wouldn't disturb the others. They sat up until midnight, and then Fury roused Nash and Oakley, who had the second shift. Laurel and Pate would finish up the night later on.

"Everything quiet?" Nash asked as Fury got ready to roll up in his blankets.

"Quiet as can be," replied Fury truthfully. Now that the wind had died down, the night was almost eerily silent. The air was still frigid, maybe even colder than the previous two nights. But Fury had a feeling tomorrow would bring a return of better weather.

He dozed off with the ease and quickness of a man who knew the importance of getting sleep whenever the chance arose. Fury's slumber was deep and dreamless.

When he came awake, it was instantly, with every nerve alert for danger.

He lay without moving, not wanting to betray the fact he was awake just yet. Something had roused him, and he wanted to know what it was before stirring. Through slitted eyes, he saw that the sky was still black overhead, although there was a faint lessening of the darkness, a tinge of gray that spoke of the approaching dawn.

"I'll scream," said Laurel Whitelaw.

"You do, and I'll kill Fury and your brothers. Come on, it ain't goin' to hurt you."

The second voice belonged to Lester Oakley. Fury turned his head just enough to see Oakley and Laurel standing on the far side of the fire. Oakley's big hands were clamped on Laurel's shoulders, trying to pull her closer to him. Nash and Frank were rolled up in their blankets, sound asleep from the looks of it, and Pate was asleep, too, sitting huddled in his coat and leaning back against one of the rocks. He was supposed to be standing guard while Laurel took care of the fire, but obviously he had dozed off. Oakley must have woken up and taken advantage of the opportunity to make advances toward Laurel.

Fury was about to roll out of his blankets as Laurel struggled to get away from Oakley. Before he could move, though, the sounds must have penetrated Pate Whitelaw's sleep-numbed brain. His head jerked up, and an angry cry ripped out of his throat as he leaped to his feet and threw himself toward Oakley.

"Leave my sister alone, you bastard!" shouted Pate as he tackled Oakley. The impact knocked Oakley's grip loose, and Laurel staggered back away from him. Pate and Oakley went down, landing hard on the cold ground.

Pate was on top. He looped wild punches at Oakley's head, but the older man blocked them and drove up a blow of his own. It caught Pate on the jaw and knocked him sprawling. Oakley went after him with a roar of rage.

Fury whipped his blankets aside and surged onto his feet. Nash and Frank were awake now, too; Frank was sitting up and looking around groggily, trying to see what the trouble was, while Nash had come up in a crouch, his right hand hovering over the butt of his gun. He straightened slowly without drawing the weapon when he saw the struggling figures of Pate and Oakley on the ground.

Oakley went after Pate's neck, trying to wrap his fingers around the boy's throat, but Pate still had his wits about him. His knee came up sharply, catching Oakley in the groin. Oakley screamed and fell to the side, but he wasn't totally distracted by the agony that nearly doubled him over. With one hand, he caught Pate's coat and jerked the boy toward him. Oakley butted him in the face. Blood spurted from Pate's nose.

The pain seemed to drive Pate into a frenzy. Again he hammered punches at Oakley's face, and this time the blows were more accurate. In a matter of instants, Oakley's nose was bleeding, too, and Laurel let out a scream as both of the fighters got to their feet and shook their heads, sending crimson droplets spraying around them. They came together like a couple of bulls charging each other.

Nash met Fury's eyes across the fire. He didn't know what the fight was about, but clearly he was hesitant to interfere. Fury felt the same way. Pate had been responsible for keeping an eye on the camp, and this trouble had started because he had dozed off. He ought to have the chance to set it right, Fury decided, at least within reason.

Pate was a well-built youngster, and he was fighting like a demon. But Oakley was older, heavier, and wilier, a veteran of many more brawls than Pate. Oakley stood up to the punishment as the two of them slugged it out, landing fewer blows than Pate, but packing more power behind each one of them than Pate did.

Finally one of Oakley's punches, a looping right hand, landed cleanly on Pate's jaw. Pate was lifted into the air, then dropped heavily on his back by the blow. He lay there, stunned. Oakley's face contorted with hate and anger, and he took a quick step forward and lifted his foot, ready to drive the heel of his boot down into Pate's face.

Fury's gun whispered out of its holster and the sound of the hammer being drawn back was clearly audible. "That's enough," he said, his voice as cold as the air around them.

Oakley stiffened, and for a second, Fury thought he was going to stomp the boy anyway. Then he lowered his foot grudgingly and growled over his shoulder, "The boy started it. He went crazy and jumped me for no damn reason!"

"That's a lie," said Fury. "I saw you molesting Miss Whitelaw, Oakley, and you're lucky I don't shoot you down like a dog."

"Take it easy, Fury," snapped Nash. His fingers twitched like he wanted to pull his own gun, but he left the revolver where it was in his holster. "We were all asleep. You can't be sure exactly what happened."

"I saw enough to know. Your partner had his hands on Laurel, and she was trying to get away from him."

"Maybe she led him on and then tried to change her mind." Nash shrugged. "It's still mighty cold. Could be she wanted some warmin' up."

"You son of a bitch!" cried Frank. "I ought to shoot you myself for saying that!"

Laurel had hurried over to Pate and knelt beside him, cradling his head in her lap. He was coming around now, blinking his eyes and shaking his head a little from side to side. Laurel brushed his hair out of his eyes and then looked up to say, "That's not true, Mr. Nash. I told your friend to leave me alone, but he just wouldn't do it."

Nash looked over at Oakley. "Lester?"

Oakley just shrugged his burly shoulders and looked down at the ground. "I was just funnin' with her," he said. "I wouldn't 've really done anything."

Fury didn't believe that for a second, but Nash seemed to. "All right," Nash said sternly. "I think you'd better apologize to the young lady." He looked at Laurel. "That satisfy you, Miss Whitelaw?"

"I . . . I suppose. If he'll promise not to do it again."

"What about you, Fury?" asked Nash. "How about puttin' up that gun and lettin' Lester say he's sorry?"

"Let's have the apology first," said Fury.

Nash nodded. "Go ahead, Lester."

Oakley shuffled over closer to Laurel and Pate. He hung his head and said, "I'm mighty sorry, Miss Whitelaw. I shouldn't ought to've bothered you, and I give you my word it won't happen again."

"All right," said Laurel, her voice still a little shaky. "I accept your apology."

Nash looked at Fury, and Fury holstered his gun. "Next time I'll kill you, Oakley," he said.

"Won't be no next time," Oakley muttered.

Fury hoped that was true. He looked at the sky again, saw that the grayness had grown. "No point in anybody going back to sleep," he said, the words accompanied by the usual clouds of fog in the cold air. "We might as well get ready to ride."

Laurel and Frank got Pate to his feet and helped him closer to the fire, where he sat down cross-legged. Laurel wet a cloth and cleaned as much of the blood as she could from his face. Oakley was doing the same thing on the other side of the fire, putting as much distance as he could between himself and the others. Fury tended to his dun and the other saddle horses while Nash went to get water from the creek.

While Nash was gone, Fury noticed for the first time that a breeze was blowing from the south again. As cold as the air was, the slight wind still cut right through a man, but the direction it came from was what was important. Warmer weather was on the way back.

By the time the group finished breakfast and had the horses saddled and ready to go, the sun was about to peek over the horizon. Oakley had kept to himself, his round face set in surly lines. That was all right with Fury; he didn't want anything to do with Oakley at the moment.

They put out the fire and left the camp, riding back down to the Brazos. There was a narrow strip of land between the river and the bluff, wide enough for the riders and the horse herd as long as the animals didn't bunch up too much. Fury saw a thin skim of ice on the surface of the Brazos; that was how cold it had been.

As he had suspected, the sun seemed to pack more heat when it rose today. The air began to warm up, and the thaw was intensified by the south wind. By midday, Fury and the others had unbuttoned their coats.

The improving weather even had the horses feeling friskier. Fury had to hold the dun back to keep it from racing ahead of the herd. Given that, it was not surprising that they made good time and covered quite a few miles during the day. After being holed up for two days, it felt damned good for everyone to stretch their legs again.

There were more hills and ridges along the river now. Some of the bluffs were covered with trees, while others were rocky and stark and mostly bare of vegetation. The river itself was shallower, and there were places where long sand bars stuck up out of the water. When they finally did cross the Brazos, Fury thought, it probably wouldn't be too difficult. There were plenty of fords where the horses wouldn't even have to swim. The biggest obstacles would be patches of quicksand in the river bed; they would have to watch out for those.

When Nash signaled for a halt, they were near a big curve in the river that was watched over on both sides by a pair of tall hills. "One or two of us can ride up there in the mornin'," Nash said, nodding toward the rise on the near bank. "Be a good place to take a look around, see what we can see. Might be able to spot some smoke from a Comanche cooking fire from up there."

It sounded like a good idea to Fury, and he said as much. He went on, "If we don't find anything tomorrow, I think we ought to cross the river and head west."

Nash nodded. "Yep. That's just what we'll do."

Fury had expected at least a little argument from the man, but Nash seemed to be in an agreeable mood today. Probably because of the change in the weather, thought Fury.

As they made camp and Laurel got their supper cooking over the fire, Fury checked their supplies. Enough for another week maybe, he decided. They had been out almost that long, and if they didn't find the Indians who were holding Felicia prisoner pretty soon, they stood a good chance of running out of provisions. Of course, there was plenty of game around, so they wouldn't starve. And they had more than enough ammunition left, having used very little of it so far. But if they ran out of things like coffee, salt, sugar, and flour, life was going to get more unpleasant. They'd survive, but they would miss those small comforts.

The dun was still saddled; Fury had left that task until last, just in case he needed to ride out again and try to bag a deer or some jackrabbits for the cooking pot. Laurel already had bacon sizzling in a pan, though, so he went to the dun and loosened the cinch around the horse's middle. That done, he took down the saddlebags.

Suddenly he paused, then unstrapped one of the pouches and slipped his hand inside. His fingers touched the butt of a small, sidehammer pocket pistol made by Henry Deringer of Philadelphia. The barrel was only two inches long, but it fired a .41-caliber ball, giving it plenty of stopping power at short range— and anybody who tried to use one of the little pistols except at short range was a damned fool. Still, it had come in handy for Fury several times since he had picked it up in New Orleans, winning it in a poker game from a big Kentucky riverboat man who had gotten tired of a run of bad luck and decided that Fury must be bottom-dealing. That had led to a nice brawl which had involved nearly everybody in the place and wrecked the bar. Fury had come out of it with a few cuts and bruises, a bump on his head, and the Deringer.

A smile plucked at his mouth as he remembered that ruckus. He was not a man who believed in portents and omens, but maybe there was a reason he had thought of the Deringer right now and checked to make sure it was still where he had stowed it. His back was to the campfire as he followed his impulse and tucked the pistol behind his belt, where it would be hidden by his coat. It was unloaded at the moment, but he could load it later, when he visited the bushes after supper. He knew from experience the gun would slide easily into the top of his boot.

Nash was still unusually affable during supper, but Oakley continued sulking. He sat by himself and said nothing as he ate. Laurel seemed to have forgotten the events of the early morning, but Fury knew from the occasional sidelong glances she gave at Oakley that she hadn't forgotten at all. Neither had Pate. His nose was swollen and bruised, as was Oakley's, but both of them had been lucky. Neither man's nose was broken.

The night would still be cold, but nowhere near as chilly as the last three nights. Fury hoped it would pass quietly. The guard shifts were rearranged slightly; Laurel would stand the first watch with him, Pate and Frank would take the second, and Nash and Oakley would finish out the night.

Laurel was quiet and pensive, saying little to him during their shift. He didn't know if she was thinking about Felicia or about the fact that she was out here dozens of miles from her home, in the middle of a wilderness ruled by Indians and outlaws. That was enough to make anyone a little nervous—especially a sixteen-year-old girl.

Pate and Frank took over at midnight, and Fury rolled into his blankets to get some much-needed sleep. He found that he didn't drop off right away as usual, however. Instead, he stared up at the sky for a while and wondered if they had all come out here on a fool's errand. Felicia Whitelaw was probably dead already; most likely had been since a day or two after the Indians had kidnapped her. There was just enough chance she was still alive, though, that they had to try to find her.

Fury dozed off, but his sleep was restless, filled with vague nightmares that faded away instantly whenever he came half-awake and shifted around. Something was bothering him, but he was damned if he could figure out what.

He found out soon enough—when he woke in the cold, gray light of dawn with the hard metal ring of a gun barrel pressed against his head and a harsh voice commanding, "Don't move, you son of a bitch, or I'll scatter your brains all over this ground!"

CHAPTER
14
· · · · · · · · · · · · · · · · · · · ·

Fury did like the gunman said—he didn't move.

Even though the words were hoarse and strained, he recognized the voice. It belonged to Bob Nash, and somehow that didn't come as any big surprise to Fury. His instincts had been warning him all along about Nash and Oakley. He had been hoping he was wrong about the two men, but all the same, he had been convinced they were just biding their time, waiting for the right moment to strike to pull off some plan they had.

That time had come, obviously.

Fury's eyes shifted, and he spotted Nash looming over him, blocking out some of the dawn sky. He felt like cursing. Nash never should have gotten close enough to him to put a gun to his head. Exhaustion must have dulled Fury's senses for Nash to get the drop on him.

"Don't bother reaching for your gun," grated Nash. "It's gone, and so's that pig sticker of yours. Now I'm goin' to back off a little, and you're goin' to sit up nice and slow and easy, understand?"

Fury's head moved in a miniscule nod.

The crouching Nash moved away from him, but the gun barrel still pointed at Fury's head. It never wavered. Fury sat up as Nash straightened.

Oakley stood on the other side of the fire with a shotgun in his hands, covering Laurel, Pate, and Frank. All three of them were still wrapped up in their blankets and appeared to be asleep. That had to be the case, Fury decided. If they were dead already, Oakley wouldn't have bothered holding the shotgun on them.

"Got their guns, Lester?" asked Nash.

"You bet," replied Oakley. "They're all sleepin' like babies. Never felt a thing."

"Good. Neither did Fury here." Nash grinned. "I'm a little disappointed in you, Fury. I figured you'd put up more of a fight than this."

"Go to hell," Fury snapped, but he knew he was just wasting his breath.

Nash didn't bother being offended. Without taking his eyes off Fury, he said to Oakley, "Wake up the rest of 'em, Lester."

"Right." Oakley stepped forward, kicked both Pate and Frank, then hopped back and brought the shotgun to bear on them again.

"Hey!" yelled Frank, thrashing in his blankets, and Pate also let out a startled exclamation. Both young men sat up abruptly, but they froze when they saw Oakley menacing them with the scattergun.

Disturbed by the commotion, Laurel rolled over and opened her eyes. Fury had to give her credit for not screaming when she saw Oakley standing there, leering and pointing a shotgun at her and her brothers. She blinked rapidly for a couple of seconds, then pushed herself into a sitting position and coolly waited to see what was going to happen.

"I reckon all of you are wonderin' what this is all about," Nash said.

Fury shook his head. "No. You're going to kill us and steal Whitelaw's horses. I figured that out right away."

Nash laughed, an ugly sound that held no genuine humor. "Not hardly," he boasted. "That's what a couple of small-timers would do, ain't it, Lester?"

"Yeah," agreed Oakley, chuckling. "Small-timers."

"We've got bigger plans in mind. We're goin' to wind up with all those horses—and the other two thousand dollars Whitelaw promised us for bringin' back his daughter."

"You sound mighty sure you're going to find those Indians who kidnapped her," said Fury. He wanted to keep Nash talking. As long as the man was gloating, he was too busy to start killing.

"Indians," repeated Nash, then laughed again. Oakley joined him. Both of them seemed to think the whole thing was hilarious.

"Findin' Felicia Whitelaw won't be any problem," Nash went on. He looked at Fury with evil triumph shining in his narrow eyes. "She's been locked up in the root cellar back at our ranch all along."

"What?" Laurel cried. Her brothers echoed her astonishment.

Fury didn't say anything, but the enormity of Nash's scheme burst on him like a bombshell. It had to have been Nash's idea, Fury decided; Oakley lacked the intelligence to come up with anything so twisted. As Fury's mind went back over everything he had seen and done since coming to this part of Texas, he saw where he had taken each wrong turn, arrived at each wrong conclusion.

"There weren't ever any Indians, were there?" he asked.

"Oh, there's plenty of Indians in these parts, all right," said Nash. "I reckon we've been lucky we haven't run into any of them, but that was a risk we had to take if we wanted everything to look right. And it had to look right if we were goin' to keep on usin' this plan like before."

"This isn't the first time you've done it, then," Fury said heavily.

"Nope. Worked just fine the first two times, too, and I reckon it will again. We'll wait a couple of years, just to make sure nobody's suspicious, maybe even move on somewhere else before we try again. But I don't see any reason why it won't keep workin'."

Pate exclaimed, "What the hell is he talking about?"

Fury looked over at the youngsters. "It wasn't Indians who kidnapped your sister," he told them. "It was white men dressed up like Indians, just in case somebody saw them besides Nash and Oakley here."

"White men?" repeated Laurel.

"White men working for Nash," Fury said. "Outlaws."

"But . . . but that's crazy!" said Frank.

"Not crazy," said Fury, looking coldly at Nash's grinning face. "Evil. Evil, but smart . . ."

"Damn right," said Nash. "The boys attacked at twilight, when everything was too shadowy for the girl to get a good look at them before they whipped a blindfold over her eyes. My wife taught 'em enough Comanche lingo that they could get by without talkin' any English around her. Like I said, they blindfolded her, rode her around in circles for a few hours so that she wouldn't have any idea where she was, then took her to my ranch and put her in the cellar. Come tomorrow, they'll take her out, still blindfolded, and bring her up this way to rendezvous with Lester and me. We turn over the horses, they give us the gal, and we head back to Waco to collect that money from her pa."

"And meanwhile your men dispose of the horses for a healthy profit, too."

Nash nodded. "You got it, Fury. It's a hell of a nice scheme— or at least it would've been if you and these young'uns hadn't horned in."

"Because now you've got to kill us."

"Damn right," Oakley said. "And I'm goin' to enjoy killin' *you*, Fury." He looked at Nash. "Can we keep the girl alive for a while, Bob, can we? Might as well enjoy her comp'ny while we're waitin' for the other fellas."

"We'll see, Lester, we'll see," promised Nash.

"Why did you wait until now?" asked Fury.

"Wanted to make sure we were far enough away from Waco that we weren't liable to run into anybody who'd recognize any of us," Nash replied. "That damn norther made things more complicated, too. Lester and I figured we'd better keep you alive for a while, just in case the weather got real bad and we needed some help."

Moving slowly so as not to spook Nash, Fury raised his left hand to rub his temples as if he had a headache. As a matter of fact, his skull *was* pounding, but that wasn't the real reason for the move. At the same time, he slipped his right hand closer to his boot under the blankets.

He had to keep Nash talking a little longer, had to buy some time by goading the man on to more boasting. He said, "When I was riding with the Rangers and trying to trail those so-called Indians, we found a spot where some shod horses crossed their path. You had a man waiting there with fresh mounts, didn't you? Your men got on shod horses while the fella who was waiting there took the Indian ponies off somewhere else."

"Good guessin'," confirmed Nash. "That's exactly what happened. Bet you don't know about the two men who got killed in the raid, though."

Fury shook his head. "No, I didn't. There were no bodies out there where we found the buggy."

"That's because Lester and I had to get rid of them before we went foggin' into Waco to spread the word. Tossed 'em in a gully and caved in the bank on 'em. Wasn't much of a burial, but we didn't have much time. Did the best we could."

The sheer cold-bloodedness of the scheme made Fury sick. He ignored the feelings in his gut and went on, "You really took care of everything, didn't you, Nash?"

"Yeah, until Whitelaw crossed us up by insistin' that you and his boys come along. We knew then we'd have to kill the three of you sooner or later, of course, but we could always say we got hit by another band of renegades while we were lookin' for Felicia. Might've looked a little bad, the three of you dyin' while Lester and I made it through, but nobody would've been able to prove anything. Most folks wouldn't have even suspected anything was wrong. They'd've just figured we were real heroes for takin' such risks to get the girl back."

In a shaky voice, Laurel said, "Then I showed up."

Nash shrugged. "That don't really change anything. We'll claim we never even saw you, and there won't be anybody around to say different. Your daddy'll think you came after us but that something happened to you before you ever caught up with us. Again, folks may wonder, but there won't be any proof."

"I'm glad Joshua and Felicia managed to kill at least two of you," said Pate. "At least not all of you will get away with this."

"Those two don't matter," Nash said callously. "I can always find more hardcases to ride for me."

"You claim Felicia's been in that root cellar all this time," said Fury.

"That's right."

"And your men have been leaving her alone?"

"Nobody's been near her 'cept my wife. She brings the girl her food and water. When I recover a prisoner from the redskins, I bring 'em back unharmed. That way her folks kind of keep on feelin' like they're in my debt. Comes in handy sometimes."

Obviously, Nash had thought everything through and then honed his scheme the first two times he and Oakley had used it. When everything went right, it was a plan that would produce healthy profits for the two of them and their accomplices without much killing. The victims had to endure a week or so of fear and torment, but they were released without any physical damage. Fury had no doubt that that wasn't from any soft-heartedness on Nash's part; it was just good business, as Nash had said.

But in this case, things hadn't worked out, and an extra four people would have to die before Nash and Oakley could receive their payoff. Obviously, they weren't going to let that stand in their way.

Fury's fingertips brushed the butt of the Deringer he had hidden in his boot the night before. It was loaded, and all it needed was to be cocked and fired. Nash was well within range . . .

"You're nothing but a couple of no-good bastards," Pate said angrily. "Too lazy to make an honest living, and too cowardly to face anybody on equal terms!"

"Keep talkin', boy," drawled Nash. "Won't do you no good, and could be you'll make Lester so mad he'll go ahead and pull one of the triggers on that greener."

"Yeah," agreed Oakley, "but you scoot away from him first, girlie. Wouldn't want any of this buckshot messin' up that pretty white skin of yours 'fore I get to know you good."

Frank Whitelaw suddenly started to his feet, and Oakley swung the barrels of the shotgun toward him. "No, Frank!" shouted Pate, reaching out to grab his brother and pull him back down. Oakley's back was hunched as he crouched over, ready to fire.

Nash's gaze left Fury long enough to dart over toward the others. In that instant, Fury closed his fingers over the Deringer and slid it smoothly out of his boot.

"Do it, Lester!" snapped Nash. "Get it over with!"

He jerked his head around to face Fury again, his finger whitening on the trigger of his Colt.

Fury fired the Deringer, right through the blanket.

CHAPTER
15

. . . .

Nash's gun went off a split second after the surprisingly loud boom of the Deringer, but in that instant the .41-caliber ball from the little pistol had slammed into his left arm, throwing off his aim. His shot went wild as he staggered back a step, the bullet missing Fury by several yards.

Fury hadn't been able to aim; it was luck and instinct that guided his shot. He dropped the now empty Deringer and flung his blankets aside as he sprang to his feet and leaped toward Nash.

At the same time, Pate Whitelaw came up off the ground and plunged toward Oakley, reaching desperately for the barrel of the shotgun as he did so. His fingers caught it and forced it down as Oakley howled a curse and jerked the first trigger.

One of the barrels of the weapon belched smoke and flame, and Pate screamed in pain as he went down. He hadn't knocked the barrels out of line enough to completely avoid the charge of buckshot.

"Run, Laurel!" Frank shouted at his sister. He was on his feet, too, darting to his left as he saw Laurel roll to the right. Oakley still had one barrel left in the shotgun, and Frank wanted to draw his fire.

That was exactly what happened. The shotgun boomed again, and Frank was thrown forward by the impact of the shot. He landed hard on the ground, rolled over a couple of times, then lay motionless. Oakley dropped the empty shotgun, yanked his pistol from its holster, and spun around to look for Laurel.

Meanwhile, Fury was struggling with Nash. With his left hand, he grabbed Nash's right wrist and wrenched it to the side so that Nash couldn't get another shot at him. Then he slammed his clubbed right fist into the wound high on the outside of Nash's left arm. Nash screamed thinly at the pain of the blow. Fury

101

chopped another punch at the man's face while Nash tried to bring the pistol back into line.

Nash was shaken by the gunshot wound, and Fury was stronger than he was. Nash kicked out at Fury's groin. Fury twisted to one side, taking most of the blow on his thigh, but enough of its force landed on the target to make him suddenly queasy and dizzy. Nash's left arm didn't work very well, but he managed to jab a couple of weak blows at Fury's head, just enough to distract him.

Fury's grasp slipped on Nash's wrist. There wasn't time to lower his arm and fire a shot at Fury; instead Nash slashed at Fury with the weapon. The barrel glanced off Fury's head. If the blow had landed solidly, it would have crushed his skull, but as it was, the gun barrel had enough force behind it to send pain lancing through Fury's brain. A red haze seemed to drop down abruptly and cover his eyes, so that everything he saw was bloody and distorted.

He swung a looping punch, knowing that if he didn't finish this fight quickly, Nash would get the better of him. That would mean sure death.

Nash jerked aside from the blow and swung the gun again, this time backhanded. The barrel caught Fury on the jaw, opening up a gash. Fury staggered. He was stronger, and a more experienced brawler than Nash. But Nash was fighting with the strength and desperation of a madman.

Across the fire, Oakley ignored the writhing figure of Pate and the still form of Frank. He ran after Laurel, reaching for her with the hand that didn't hold a gun. His fingers caught the collar of her coat and fastened firmly on it. Digging in his heels, Oakley jerked her to a halt. Laurel stumbled, pulled off her feet. She would have fallen if it had not been for Oakley's grip on her coat.

Fury saw the barrel of Nash's gun sweeping toward him again and knew that this time it would deal death. He lowered his head and dove forward, tackling Nash around the middle. The gun boomed just above and beside his head. The sound smashed into his ear like a fist, deafening him on that side.

That was the least of his worries. He might well be dead before he had a chance to find out if his hearing was going to come back or not.

Fury and Nash sprawled to the ground, Fury once again searching for a grip on Nash's wrist. Nash wound up on top. He lifted the gun, ready to bring it crashing down on Fury's head.

Somehow, Nash's hat had stayed on his head during the fight. Now it suddenly went sailing off. At almost the same instant, dust geysered from the ground next to Fury's ear as a bullet plowed into the dirt. Across the clearing, a frightened Oakley howled, "Somebody's shootin' at us!"

Fury took advantage of Nash's momentary distraction to hurl the man off him and roll away. More slugs thudded into the ground nearby. Oakley dropped Laurel and ducked toward the cover of some trees as shots whined around his head.

"They're gonna kill us!" he cried.

Fury didn't know what the hell was going on, but one thing was certain—with all the lead buzzing around, this wasn't a safe place to be. He leaped to his feet and raced over to Laurel, who had pushed herself to her hands and knees. Fury grabbed her arm and pulled her up.

A slug sang past, close to the ear that was still working. He flinched instinctively from it and then gave Laurel a shove. "Get into the trees!" he told her.

Nash was spinning around crazily, looking for the source of the gunfire that had plucked his hat right off his head. Not finding anything, he ran for cover, too, crashing into the underbrush after Oakley.

Laurel was heading the other way, toward the river. Fury cast a glance after her, then ran over to Pate, who was struggling to get to his feet. The right leg of his pants was soaked with blood from the knee down. Fury caught him under the arms and lifted him. "Can you run?" he asked.

"I can damn sure *hop!*" replied the injured youngster.

"Then go after your sister. I'll tend to Frank."

While Pate hobbled as quickly as he could toward the trees, Fury hurried over to Frank. He didn't know if the boy was even still alive, but he had to find out before he headed for cover himself. Dropping to a knee beside Frank's head, Fury pressed his fingers to the boy's neck in search of a pulse.

He found one, erratic and not very strong, but definitely there. The back of Frank's coat was stained with blood where the shotgun blast had caught him. Carefully, Fury lifted the boy and slung him over a shoulder, then started in a crouching run toward the trees where Laurel and Pate had disappeared.

The gunfire had eased up, with only the occasional crack of a rifle sounding now and then. Fury reached the trees without any more bullets coming close to him and Frank.

The underbrush was fairly thick, but Fury found a path through it. No doubt the trail had been widened a little by Pate and Laurel crashing through it. Fury didn't hear any noise up ahead, or anywhere else around, for that matter. The Whitelaws had probably gone to ground, as had Nash and Oakley.

"Mr. Fury!"

Laurel hissed his name from a thicket. Fury veered in that direction and saw the girl motioning to him while she held back some of the brush with her other hand. He trotted through the opening, beginning to breathe hard now from the effort of toting Frank around.

On the other side of the screening vegetation, the ground sloped down into a shallow, natural bowl that was encircled by bushes. Not a bad hiding place, thought Fury, knowing it was lucky Laurel and Pate had stumbled on it. Pate was waiting at the bottom of the slope, sitting on the ground with his wounded leg stretched out in front of him.

"Frank . . . ?" he asked in a low, anxious voice.

"He's alive," Fury told him as he carefully and gently lowered Frank to the ground next to Pate. "Don't know how bad he's hurt, but he was still breathing a minute ago. How are you doing?"

"I'll be all right," replied Pate. His face was washed out and his voice was shaky, though, despite his claim. "That buckshot chewed up my calf pretty good, but I think it missed the bone. I've lost some blood, but I'll be fine."

Fury glanced at Laurel. She was still crouched behind the brush at the top of the rise, keeping watch. Fury said to Pate, "You'll have to give me a hand with your brother."

Pate nodded grimly. "Whatever you say."

Fury eased the unconscious Frank into a sitting position next to Pate and said, "See if you can get his coat and shirt off while I hold him up."

Fighting his own weakness, Pate went to work. He struggled to remove Frank's coat, and when he finally had that off, both he and Fury could see how bloody the youngster's shirt was. The bleeding seemed to have stopped, however. Fury held Frank upright with one hand and unbuttoned his shirt with the other, then Pate removed the garment.

Fury shifted around so that he could survey the damage to Frank's back. After a moment, he grunted, more satisfied than he had expected to be.

"Oakley was too slow on the trigger or too quick, whichever way you want to look at it," said Fury. "Frank got far enough away so that the charge had spread out some, and with Oakley not waiting until the barrel was lined up, just the edge of the blast caught Frank here."

There were only three wounds in Frank's back where the buckshot had penetrated. Fury couldn't tell how deep they were. Frank had bled quite a bit and passed out from the shock, but sometimes even the messiest wounds weren't that serious if they were tended to soon enough. The boy was beginning to moan and stir around a little, so Fury settled him back down on his side.

"Let's take a look at that leg of yours," he said to Pate.

He had no knife to cut the denim, so he had to tear it back. The tough fabric parted grudgingly, but eventually Fury had Pate's leg exposed. From the blood that had collected in Pate's boot, Fury expected the injuries to be severe, and he saw he was right. The buckshot had shredded the flesh of Pate's calf, and it was a miracle the bone wasn't broken. The bleeding had slowed down but not stopped completely. Pate tore strips off the tail of his shirt, and Fury bound them tightly around the wounded leg. Pate was shivering now. The air was still cold this morning, and he would be chilled by the loss of blood, too.

When Fury had the wound bandaged as well as he could, he looked up and noticed that the sun had risen and its light was beginning to slant down through the underbrush into the bowl where they were hidden. It seemed like hours had passed since he had been awakened by the touch of Nash's gun barrel, but he knew that less than an hour had really gone by.

Frank was half conscious now. Fury put a hand on his shoulder and said quietly, "Lie still, son. If you move around much, you'll get those wounds to bleeding again."

"M-Mr. Fury . . . ?" muttered Frank. "Am . . . am I going to die?"

"Not from those scratches on your back," Fury assured him. "Better keep quiet, though, until we find out who was doing all that shooting earlier." He looked at Pate and said, "Are you all right to stay here and keep an eye on your brother?"

Pate swallowed hard. "Sure," he said, his voice firm but betrayed somewhat by the haggard lines etched into his pale face.

Fury nodded and slapped him on the shoulder, then scrambled up the slope to join Laurel. As he crouched next to her, he asked in a whisper, "See anything out there?"

She shook her head. "No sign of Nash or Oakley, and I haven't heard them moving around, either." She looked over at him. "Mr. Fury, could you tell where that shooting was coming from earlier?"

"The south, I think, but I never saw who was doing it. The way it worked out, they picked a mighty handy time to cut loose at us. Sure scared off Nash and Oakley."

"But now we're sitting here with no guns and no horses." Laurel's voice trembled a little as she summed up their situation.

Fury shrugged. "We're still alive. That's better than it could have been."

There had not been any more shooting for quite a while. Eventually, Fury knew, he would have to move out of hiding and see if it was safe for the others to emerge.

"How are Pate and Frank?" Laurel asked anxiously.

"I think they'll both be all right if we're not stuck out here in the middle of nowhere for too long."

"We can't stay here. We have to get back to Waco and save Felicia."

"Your sister's going to be all right," Fury told her confidently. "She's worth a couple of thousand dollars to Nash and Oakley, so she's in no danger from them."

"What if both of them are dead, though?" Laurel wanted to know. "What will the rest of that . . . that gang do with her?"

That was a question Fury couldn't answer. He just looked at Laurel and shook his head.

Before either of them could say anything else, a faint sound caught Fury's attention. He lifted his head, listening intently.

After a moment, he identified the noise as hoofbeats. Someone was riding toward their position from the south, the same direction as the gunshots had come from. Fury motioned for Laurel to be quiet and urged her to crouch lower to the ground. He did the same thing, hunkering down until he was completely concealed by the brush. He looked over his shoulder at Pate and Frank and put a finger to his lips, signaling them to be silent as well. From the steadily growing sound of the hoofbeats, quite a few riders were approaching the spot where Fury and the others had been camped.

Fury moved a couple of branches aside just enough for him to see through the gap he had created. Beside him, Laurel did the same thing. Fury spotted the riders first. He felt a surge of surprise go through him, and he hoped Laurel wouldn't gasp in shock when she saw them.

The men riding on sturdy ponies wore buckskins and had their heads shaved in scalplocks. They carried an assortment of muskets and breech-loaders, old guns for the most part, but well taken care of and still quite deadly. Fury recognized the grim-faced warriors immediately.

Cherokees.

He thought he recognized a few of them from that village he had visited along with Captain Sprague and the other Texas Rangers. But what were those Indians doing way up here, thirty or forty miles from their home? And why had they opened fire on the campsite?

Beside him, Laurel stiffened as the Indians came into her field of view. Quickly, Fury put a hand on her arm to warn her not to cry out.

He looked back at the Cherokees. They were sagging on the backs of their unshod mounts, and the ponies themselves seemed exhausted, as if they had been running for a long time. Fury made a rough count of the group, arriving at a figure of just under three dozen. A sizable bunch, but not nearly all the inhabitants of that Cherokee village southwest of Waco, if that was indeed where these men were from. Most of the riders were young, and their faces were painted for war.

Vivid images of the slaughtered Cherokee hunting party sprang into Fury's mind. That massacre was bound to have been discovered by now. Could some of the younger Cherokees have reacted to the killings by leaving the village and going on a murder raid in retaliation? They might have hit Waco itself or at least some of the surrounding ranches and farms, then lit out along the Brazos toward the wild country to the northwest, hoping to escape the vengeance of the white settlers. That would explain what these braves were doing here, and it would also explain why they had opened fire on the camp. A war party like that would attack any whites they happened to encounter.

Those thoughts raced through Fury's mind in a matter of instants, and he was convinced his hastily formed theory was correct. If he was right, the Indians would be moving on, and all he and his companions needed to do was lie low until the Cherokees were gone. Then they could look for their horses, try to get Pate and Frank to a place where they could receive medical attention, and deal with the continuing threat of the murderous Nash and Oakley.

That was all, thought Fury with a bleak smile plucking at his mouth.

This time, Laurel grabbed his arm to alert him to something, instead of the other way around. She was peering through the bushes, and she gestured frantically with her other hand. Fury crouched a little more and squinted through the screen of foliage again.

Another handful of Indians had come along, trailing a little way behind the main group. One of these braves was leading a horse, and perched on the back of the animal was a young woman with long, tangled blonde hair. Her wrists were lashed together in front of her. She hung on tightly to the pony's mane so that she wouldn't be unseated as the Cherokee jerked her mount along. Even at this distance, Fury could see that her eyes were wide and terrified.

And from the stunned, horrified expression on Laurel's face, he knew without being told that he was looking right at Felicia Whitelaw.

CHAPTER
16

· ·

Fury's mind was spinning. If Nash and Oakley had been telling the truth when they were gloating about their scheme—and they had no reason to lie, as far as Fury could see—then how the hell had Felicia wound up here as the captive of a band of renegade Cherokees? She was supposed to be back at the ranch near Waco, stashed in that root cellar.

The answer suggested itself almost immediately, and it supported Fury's assumption that these Indians were on the run after a revenge raid. The ranch where Felicia had been held prisoner must have been one of the places the Cherokees had hit. Nash's Comanche wife might be dead now, since Fury didn't see any other prisoners, or she might have been lucky enough to escape the vengeance of the Cherokees.

The main group of Indians had passed by far enough now that Fury thought he could take a chance. He whispered, "Is that Felicia?"

Laurel's head jerked spasmodically in a nod. Her eyes looked like those of a surprised, panic-stricken doe about to leap away in wild flight. "I don't understand . . . She . . . How . . . ?"

Fury's theory about the Cherokees was too complicated to explain in a few hurried, whispered sentences. He settled for saying, "It doesn't matter how. What's important is that we know where she is."

"But Nash and Oakley said—"

"I'd wager they don't know anything about this."

The irony of it struck Fury then. Felicia Whitelaw had been kidnapped and her brother Joshua murdered by white men pretending to be Indians. Now, through as strange a set of circumstances as Fury ever hoped to encounter, she had actually become a prisoner of the redskins. If not for the phony kidnapping, Sprague and the Rangers would not have been out looking

109

for her and would not have killed the members of that peaceful hunting party, an action which had in turn sent those young, hot-headed Cherokee braves off to raid the farms and ranches of the whites—on one of which they had found Felicia.

Fury's head was starting to hurt worse, and he didn't think it was solely from being clouted with Bob Nash's six-gun.

The Indians who had been in charge of Felicia were out of sight now, and Laurel was starting to look even more frantic. She might lose her head, jump out of the brush, and take off running after them.

"Come on," said Fury, pointing to Pate and Frank. "Let's go tell your brothers." The young men had to know about this, and telling them would keep Laurel occupied for a little while.

"Are we going to just let those . . . those savages ride off with her?"

"We don't have any choice right now," Fury replied bluntly. "But we'll get her back, Laurel. I can promise you that."

She looked dubious, like his promise didn't mean much to her anymore, if it ever had. But when he took a firm grip on her arm and started down the slope, she went with him without fighting.

"What is it?" Pate asked when they reached the bottom of the hollow, knowing from the expressions on their faces that something had happened.

"It's Felicia!" Laurel burst out. "We just saw her!"

"What?" Pate was astounded, as he had every right to be. Frank looked up at them curiously, too. He seemed to be coming back to his senses.

Fury knelt beside the two wounded young men and quickly explained the situation as he saw it, going over the details for Laurel's benefit as well as for Pate and Frank.

When Fury was finished, Pate started to push himself to his feet. "We've got to go after them," he said stubbornly.

Fury put a hand on his arm to stop him. "Like I told Laurel, we can't just go running after them like that. She'd wind up a prisoner, too, and the rest of us would be dead."

"Then what *can* we do?" asked Pate in an agonized voice.

"We can try to find out how bad your brother's hurt," said Fury. "Lie down on your stomach, Frank."

Frank complied with the order. Fury used another strip torn from Pate's shirt to clean away as much of the blood around the wounds as he could, but it was difficult without any water.

Some of the blood had already dried. None of the buckshot pellets had passed through Frank's body, so that meant they were still in there.

"This is going to hurt like hell, boy," he told Frank. "I want your brother and sister to hold you down, but it's going to be up to you not to yell out and maybe let those Indians know we're here. We can gag you if you want."

"I won't yell," Frank promised grimly.

"Hope not. All our lives could be riding on you."

Fury motioned for Pate and Laurel to take hold of Frank, and then he began probing in one of the wounds with a finger. It would have been a hell of a lot better if he'd had a knife to dig out the buckshot, but his Bowie was gone. If the pellets had penetrated very far into Frank's back, he wouldn't be able to get them.

Luckily, he touched the small lead ball a moment later. Frank bucked up a little before Pate and Laurel could tighten their grip on him. A low groan sounded deep in his throat, but that was the only noise he made.

Fury glanced up at Laurel and Pate. Both of them were pale. "Don't you two pass out," he warned. "Hang on to him now."

He began working the buckshot out and a moment later had it in the palm of his hand, a tiny, bloody ball. Fury tossed it aside and began working on the next wound.

His luck held, and ten minutes was all that was required to pry the other two pieces of buckshot out of Frank's flesh. It was a damned long ten minutes, though, made easier only by the fact that Frank passed out again about halfway through.

"Wish we had some whiskey to pour in those holes," Fury said when he was finished. "And some to clean up that leg of yours, too, Pate. Maybe we'll be lucky and none of the wounds will mortify."

"You can cut off my leg if you need to," said Pate. "I don't care as long as it helps us rescue Felicia."

Fury grinned wearily at the young man and clapped him on the shoulder. "I don't reckon we're quite at that point yet," he said. "Thanks for your help, both of you."

Laurel asked, "What about Frank? Those wounds are bleeding pretty bad again."

"Let 'em bleed," said Fury. "That'll help clean them out. We'll bandage him up in a little bit."

While Pate and Laurel were keeping an eye on Frank, Fury decided to do some looking around. He climbed back to the top of the slope and moved slowly around the bowl, studying the surrounding landscape through the brush. Nothing was moving in the vicinity of their hiding place, not even any small animals. All the wildlife had hidden during the shooting, and the creatures weren't ready to emerge again just yet.

Fury could see the campsite from where he was. Their gear was scattered around the clearing, and it looked like the Indians had paused there long enough to ransack the place and take everything of value. The horses were gone, too, and Fury wondered if they had been stolen by the Cherokees as well or if they had broken free and stampeded off when the gunfire started.

He hated to think about his dun being in the hands of the Indians. He wasn't a man to get overly sentimental about an animal, but he and the horse had been together for a long time. The dun was probably the best saddle horse he'd ever had.

If the dun was anywhere close by, a whistle from Fury would bring the horse running, but it would also alert anyone else within hearing to their presence. If Nash and Oakley had managed to hide from the Cherokees, too, and were within hearing, they would still be interested in finding Fury and the others.

Nash and Oakley still needed them dead in order for the plan to work. They might not know the Cherokees had already ruined the scheme by abducting Felicia Whitelaw.

Fury risked a dash over to the campsite to see if the Indians had left any food or other useful provisions behind. He didn't find anything. The Cherokees had taken just about everything, including the little Deringer that had helped save his life. Fury's features were set in grim lines when he returned to the hollow where Laurel, Pate, and Frank were hiding.

Frank had regained consciousness and was sitting up while Laurel tied bandages on his wounds. The shirts belonging to Pate and Frank had both been pretty well ripped up to serve as dressings for their wounds. The young men still had their coats, however, and with the weather steadily warming again, they wouldn't freeze.

"Did you see anything?" asked Pate.

Fury shook his head. "Those Cherokees are long gone, and I didn't see any sign of Nash or Oakley. That doesn't mean they're not still around here somewhere, though."

"You don't think the Indians got them?"

All Fury could do was shrug. "No way of knowing unless we run into them or find their bodies."

Laurel glanced up at Fury as she finished bandaging Frank's wounds. "What are we going to do now? We can't just sit here forever."

"No, we can't," agreed Fury. "We'll start after those Indians on foot. We know they've got horses, and we're going to have to have mounts sooner or later if we're going to get back to Waco. Pate and Frank aren't in any shape to walk that far."

"What about Felicia?" Pate asked.

"The Cherokees have her, too, so we'll deal with that when we get our hands on some horses."

"You mean we're going to rescue her when we steal those ponies?"

"Don't get ahead of yourself, boy," Fury advised. "Right now let's just worry about catching up to those redskins."

Laurel gave Frank a hand as they left the hollow. Pate's injury made it harder for him to walk, so Fury slipped an arm around the youngster's waist and supported him. Their pace was slow as they limped away from the hiding place, but it was the best they could do.

Fury led them past the campsite, all the time listening and watching intently in case Nash and Oakley—or the Cherokees— came back. They seemed to be alone here in this wilderness, not another human soul within a hundred miles, but Fury knew that wasn't true. Probably less than five miles away, there were plenty of people. People who wanted him and his companions dead.

Judging from the sun, it was not quite mid-morning. This had already been a long day, and it was going to get longer still. None of them had eaten since the night before, so when Fury spotted a tangle of wild berries on the bank of the river, he steered the other three toward them.

"The freeze probably got these berries," said Fury, "so they won't taste very good. Better than nothing, though."

He was right. The berries, which had been nowhere near ripe to start with, had been killed by the late freeze and were starting to rot. They ate them anyway, then washed them down with river water. A hell of a breakfast, thought Fury, but at least they were still alive to complain about it.

The four continued their slow pace along the Brazos while the sun climbed steadily higher. Pate and Frank tired rapidly, and Fury had to call several halts so they could rest. It was during one of those breaks when Fury heard hoofbeats and out of the corner of his eye saw movement in a nearby stand of cottonwoods.

"Down!" he hissed to the others. They crouched behind some brush while Fury waited to see who would emerge from the trees.

Suddenly a grin appeared on his tired face, and he stood up. "Come on," he said to his companions. "It's nothing to be afraid of."

He trotted into the open, letting the saddleless, riderless lineback dun see him. The horse stopped, threw up its head, and whinnied a greeting, then raced toward Fury. As it came up to him, he caught it around the neck and affectionately slapped its flank. After a moment of reunion, Fury led the horse toward Laurel and her brothers, who had emerged from the brush.

"I knew unless the Indians got him he'd still be around," said Fury. "We'll be able to make better time now. Pate, you and Frank can take turns riding."

"What about the rest of our horses?" asked Laurel.

Fury shook his head. "They probably scattered. If we run across them, though, we'll have an easier time catching them now that this old boy's back."

He ripped some of the pieces of fringe off his pants and tied them together to make a rude hackamore for the dun. When he was finished, he helped Pate onto the horse's bare back and handed the youngster the makeshift reins.

Fury's prediction was right. They were able to travel more quickly now, although Frank's wounds still made it impossible for him to move very fast. Fury was a little surprised they were moving at all, after all they had been through. Pate and Frank really needed the attentions of a good doctor and probably a couple of weeks in bed, at the very least. Instead, they were plugging along without complaint, still more interested in rescuing Felicia than they were in their own welfare.

It was that spirit that made them pioneers, thought Fury. And he was damned proud to know them.

They pushed on, following the Brazos. Fury watched the banks of the river for any sign that the Cherokees might have crossed the stream and headed west. He didn't see any tracks to indicate that, though. More than likely the Indians were doing the same thing he and his companions were—staying close to the river since it was a good source of fresh water and would also attract enough game to furnish plenty of meals.

By late afternoon, the four of them had still not seen anyone else. They hadn't eaten anything since the berries that morning, and Fury could tell that they couldn't go on much longer. When they came to an open, grassy area on the bank of the river, bounded by a thick stand of trees, Fury said, "We'll camp here tonight. Best take it easy and get some rest."

They took Fury's advice. Frank was riding the dun at the moment, so Laurel helped him down, then all three of the Whitelaws slumped to the ground in utter exhaustion.

Fury was tired, too, and his feet hurt like hell. Boots were made for riding, not walking, as he had discovered on a few other occasions. But tired or not, he still had work to do.

He went into the trees and looked for a branch of the proper size among the oaks. When he found one, he broke it off. The spot where it had broken tapered to a relatively sharp point, which was exactly what he wanted. Carrying the branch, he returned to the river and waded out into the shallows.

Laurel sat up and watched him curiously. Fury held the branch up about shoulder level and stood motionless for long minutes. Then, suddenly, with a movement so fast that Laurel's eyes could barely follow it, he thrust the branch into the water and pushed down hard with it.

When he lifted the makeshift spear, there was a fish impaled on it. A good-sized largemouth bass, from the looks of it, which wiggled and flopped for a moment before dying.

Fury pulled the fish off the pointed branch and tossed it on the bank. "See if you can find a rock with a sharp enough edge that you can gut that," he told Laurel. "I've got flint and tinder in my pocket, so we can at least have a fire." He turned and lifted the crude spear again, waiting for another unwary fish to swim past him.

The same speed of hand and eye that enabled Fury to draw and fire a pistol faster and more accurately than most men was put to good use as he speared two more bass. By that time, Laurel had found a chunk of quartz with enough of an edge on it to do a rough job of cleaning the first fish. Fury dropped the other two on the ground beside her and then went into the trees again to gather some small branches for a fire. There was still enough light in the sky from the setting sun that the flames would not be very visible for a while, and Fury intended to have the fire put out by the time darkness fell. The smoke and the smell of the burning wood might attract attention, but Fury was willing to take the chance. In their weakened condition, Pate and Frank needed some hot food.

By the time the fish had been spitted on sticks and cooked over the small campfire, the two young men were sitting up, their eyes bright with ravenous hunger. Fury divided up the fish. It wasn't much of a meal—bony, half-cooked fish—but all four of them ate eagerly and wanted more when they were through. Fury heaped sand on the little fire, though. Dusk was settling in, and they couldn't afford to let the flames burn any longer. Weaponless as they were, they would be easy pickings for anybody who wanted to ambush them.

"How far ahead of us do you think those Indians are, Mr. Fury?" asked Laurel. She sat with her legs drawn up and her arms clasped around her denim-clad knees.

"Don't know," Fury answered honestly. "They were probably moving at a pretty smart clip when they left Waco, but by now they may think they've left any pursuit a long way behind them. Could be they've slowed down some. We've got to hope so, anyway."

Pate said, "I still don't see how we're going to get Felicia and some horses away from them."

"Neither do I," grunted Fury. "But we'll figure out a way when the time comes."

"When the time comes," repeated Pate. "I don't want to sound ungrateful, Mr. Fury . . . God knows we'd all be dead now if it wasn't for you . . . but that's what you said earlier, and I just don't understand it. It seems to me like we've got have some sort of plan."

Fury found himself smiling in the darkness. He said quietly, "You may not know it now, son, but most of life is just making it up as you go along."

"That's a right peculiar attitude," said the man who stepped out of the shadows and pointed a gun at Fury.

CHAPTER
17

Fury looked up in amazement at the bearded face of Texas Ranger Captain Ben Sprague. Every muscle in Fury's body had tensed for action as Sprague stepped out of the darkness, but there was nothing he could do. Sprague had the drop on him.

But why was Sprague pointing a gun at him in the first place? They'd had their differences, but the last time Fury had checked, the two of them were on the same side. He ought to have felt a great surge of relief to have Sprague turn up.

Instead, Fury's gut told him that things were liable to get worse.

Sprague lowered the gun, though, and said, "Is that the Whitelaw younkers with you?"

"It's us, all right, Captain," answered Pate. "Lord, I hope you've got a whole troop of Rangers with you!"

"Some of the boys're ridin' with me," Sprague confirmed. "Left 'em back over yonder in the woods when we spotted your fire burnin' a few minutes ago. Figured I'd do a little scoutin'." He holstered his gun and moved closer to the four of them. As he hunkered on his heels, he pushed his battered black hat to the back of his head and looked at Laurel in the twilight. "Heard you'd run off, missy. Your pa figured you'd come after your brothers on this here rescue mission. Looks like things didn't work out too good. No guns, no food, just one horse."

"You can't take us back to Waco yet, Captain," Frank said excitedly. "We know where Felicia is. Now that you and your men are here, we can rescue her for sure."

"Didn't say nothin' about takin' anybody back to Waco," grunted Sprague. "An' we didn't come out here to rescue no prisoners, neither. We come to even the score with a bunch o' bloody-handed, red-skinned bastards."

"The Cherokees," guessed Fury.

"Damn right. Been chasin' 'em for over four days now, ever since they came maraudin' up and down the river. Killed nearly twenty folks 'fore they was through at the farms and ranches around town. I reckon we're lucky they weren't crazy enough to raid the settlement itself."

"What about our parents?" asked Laurel anxiously. "Did they attack my father's ranch?"

Sprague shook his head. "Nope, they left the Whitelaw place alone. Reckon they didn't want to run up against Jase Sutton and that salty bunch of hands your pa's got. I just wish they'd tried to hit Fort Fisher. We'd've showed 'em what for, and if they had, we sure wouldn't still be chasin' 'em clear up the Brazos like this."

"They've got Felicia Whitelaw," Fury said. "When they raided Nash and Oakley's place, they must have found her there in the root cellar."

Sprague stared at him. "How'd you know the redskins hit that ranch? And what's this about Felicia Whitelaw bein' there?"

"You'd better call your men in," Fury said grimly. "It's a long story."

Sprague frowned in thought for a moment, then nodded, stood up, and vanished once more into the gathering gloom. A few minutes later, hoofbeats sounded in the night as the company of Rangers rode out of the trees and came up to the river.

"Cold camp again tonight, boys," Sprague called to his men as he dismounted. "Break out some jerky and biscuits. I reckon these folks could sure use a little more supper."

"And some whiskey if you've got it," added Fury.

"Whiskey?"

"Pate and Frank have some gunshot wounds that need cleaning."

Sprague nodded and motioned for his lieutenant to see to it. He sat down near Fury again and said, "Now tell me what the hell this is all about."

Fury told him. He concluded by saying, "I don't know what happened to Nash and Oakley. The Cherokees could have killed them, or they could be wandering around out here somewhere, too. The important thing is those Indians aren't too far ahead of us. We can catch up to them and get Felicia Whitelaw back from them."

"*Now* you're makin' plans," Sprague said dryly. "I thought you was a big'un for figurin' it out as you go along."

Fury grinned. "Never turn down a plan that walks right into your camp."

"Yeah, well, we'll see." Sprague shook his head. "So Nash and Oakley were behind the whole thing. Never would've figured that. I never cottoned much to them two, but I didn't know 'em very well, either." His voice hardened as he went on, "Hate to say it about a couple of white men, but I almost hope them Cherokees got 'em."

With a nod, Fury said, "It'd be fitting."

He wasn't going to believe it just yet, though. Until he saw their bodies, he couldn't assume that Nash and Oakley were dead.

"We'll rest our horses here tonight," Sprague went on. "Been pushin' 'em pretty hard since we left Waco. Now that we know them redskins aren't that far ahead of us, we can afford to take a little extra time."

"What about Felicia?" asked Laurel. "Can she afford it?"

"Don't you worry none about your sister, missy," Sprague assured her gruffly.

Fury heard the insincerity in the Ranger captain's tone. He had a feeling Sprague was much more interested in vengeance against the Cherokees than he was in rescuing Felicia Whitelaw. Under the circumstances, though, maybe the two things could be combined.

Deep inside, Fury felt a strong weariness. He had been holding things together all day, keeping the Whitelaw youngsters moving and not thinking too much about their desperate situation. Now, with close to two dozen Rangers on hand, he could relax. The wounds suffered by Pate and Frank had been cleaned and rebandaged by a Ranger who'd had plenty of experience at patching up bullet wounds; there was a much better chance now that the two young men would be all right. Tomorrow, Fury could reclaim his dun, and the other three could double up with some of the men from Fort Fisher. There was probably even a spare six-gun among them that Fury could borrow. Things should have looked a lot brighter to him.

So why couldn't he shake off the bad feeling that was nagging at him?

Exhaustion played no hunches. After Fury had eaten some of

the Rangers' food, he stretched out and rolled up in a blanket Sprague loaned him, and he was asleep within minutes, a deep slumber almost like being dead.

The night passed quietly, and everyone was up early the next morning. After a cold breakfast, they saddled up and moved out, still following the Brazos.

As Fury rode alongside Sprague, the captain filled him in on more of the details of the Cherokee raid. Nash's Comanche wife had indeed been killed when the marauders hit the ranch; the Rangers had found her mutilated body beside the door to the root cellar. Had she been trying to protect Felicia when she was killed, wondered Fury, or was she merely trying to hide herself? The answer didn't really matter—she was dead now.

Also found on the ranch were the bodies of half a dozen men who had been strangers to Sprague. They must have been members of Nash's gang, Fury speculated, probably some were the same men who had pretended to be Indians when Felicia Whitelaw was kidnapped and her brother murdered.

"Why do you reckon they didn't grab Joshua, too?" mused Sprague.

Fury shrugged. "Maybe they figured he'd put up too much of a fight to bother with him. Also they had to make sure it looked like Indians had gotten Felicia in order for the plan to work, and Indians don't often take adult males as captives."

"Yeah, I reckon that makes sense. But why go to all the trouble of havin' Nash and Oakley seem to stumble onto the kidnappin' like that? They could've just rode into Waco and told their story without actually bein' there."

"Nash probably wanted to be on hand in case anything went wrong," said Fury, "like those two men who were killed. He and Oakley had to get rid of their bodies, remember? Shooting at the fake Indians was just for show, in case anybody else happened to be around. That way they'd have witnesses to prove how brave they had been, and it would sure make their story sound a lot stronger."

"Yeah," nodded Sprague, following Fury's reasoning. "Sure were a pair of tricky bastards."

"Especially Nash. I got the feeling he came up with all the ideas; Oakley just helped him carry them out."

"Don't mind sayin' it again. I hope the Cherokees caught up

with 'em. That'd save us from havin' to hunt 'em down later."

It was going to be mighty frustrating, thought Fury, if they couldn't find any evidence of what had happened to Nash and Oakley. He would hate to never know whether they were dead or alive. If they were dead, all well and good, but if they were still alive . . . If they were alive, they might turn up somewhere else on the frontier, trying to pull this same vicious scheme again. Fury didn't like the thought of that.

Sprague set a brisk pace. Fury kept an eye on Laurel, Pate, and Frank to see how they were handling it. Laurel seemed to be fine, but her brothers were both still pale and a little shaky. There had to be a limit to how far and how hard they could push themselves, wounded the way they were, but obviously they hadn't reached it yet. They didn't want to hold back the Rangers. The sooner they caught up to the Cherokees, the sooner Felicia would be safe.

Along toward noon, the group approached a hill rising to the east of the river. Sprague waved toward it and said, "Reckon a couple of us ought to ride up there and take a look around, see if we can spot them Indians. Want to go along, Fury?"

"Sure." Fury wished he still had his spyglass, but that had been looted from the campsite along with everything else in his saddlebags.

Sprague gave the order to halt, then left his second-in-command in charge while he and Fury rode up the wooded, brushy slope. It was tough going, especially now that the weather had warmed up again. Both men and both horses were sweating by the time they reached the summit.

The effort was worth it, though. The height gave them a good view of the Brazos River valley for miles. Fury's eye followed the stream as it bent and curled through the hills, and after a moment he pointed and said sharply to Sprague, "Look there."

Taking out a spyglass, Sprague extended it and lifted it to his eye. He squinted through the instrument for a moment, looking in the direction Fury had pointed, then jerked his head in a nod. "That's them, all right," he said as he handed the spyglass to Fury.

Fury focused in on the distant riders he had spotted beside the river. They seemed to leap right up to him as he peered through the spyglass. He moved his gaze along the line of Cherokees, noting that they didn't look quite so tired now. As he had thought, they probably believed themselves beyond pursuit and had slowed down a little.

The same gap was at the end of the line, with the small group of braves bringing up the rear with the prisoner. From this angle, Fury couldn't see Felicia Whitelaw's face, but from the way she sagged on the back of the pony he could tell the journey was taking a toll on her. At least she was still alive, he thought.

He had looked through the spyglass long enough. The Cherokees were riding away from the hill where he and Sprague were, but if one of the Indians happened to look back, he might spot sunlight reflecting off the lens. Fury lowered the instrument and gave it back to Sprague.

"About two miles ahead of us," Fury said. "We can close that gap."

"Yep. Don't reckon we'll hit 'em until tonight, though. I want 'em thinkin' they're nice and safe."

Just like that hunting party, thought Fury. Sprague had another ambush in mind.

"What about Felicia Whitelaw?"

Sprague just looked at him. "What about her?"

"Aren't you going to try to get her away from them first? If you don't, she's liable to be hit by a stray bullet during the fighting."

"That'd be a damned shame." Sprague leaned forward in his saddle and regarded Fury intently. "I didn't come out here to rescue that gal. Like I told you, me'n the boys came to kill Injuns. Once that's done, if the girl's still alive, I'll be right happy for her and her family. But she ain't my main concern."

Fury felt cold fingers tickling along his backbone. "You're saying you don't give a damn if she gets killed or not," he said, the words tinged with horror and contempt.

"I'm sayin' I ain't lettin' nothin' interfere with killin' them Cherokees," snapped Sprague. "I got dead Texans to avenge, mister."

"And what will Felicia be if she gets killed when you hit their camp? Just one more dead Texan for you to avenge?"

Sprague's bearded jaw tightened as Fury's bitter words lashed at him. "Don't reckon I'd expect you to understand."

"Good, because I sure as hell don't."

Sprague turned his horse. "Come on. Let's get back down with the others. We'll talk about this while we're headin' on up the river."

Fury nodded grimly. He didn't expect to be able to talk sense into Sprague, but he had to at least make the effort.

They rode down the hill to rejoin the rest of the Ranger troop. As they neared the bottom of the slope, Sprague hung back for a moment, caught in some thick brush—or so Fury thought.

He knew differently a second later when he heard the whisper of steel on leather and then the unmistakable sound of a Colt's hammer being drawn back.

Jerking the dun to a halt, Fury tried to spin around, but Sprague's voice stopped him. "Don't move, Fury," the captain said coldly. "I'd hate to shoot you, but I'd sure as hell do it if you made me."

Fury glanced over his shoulder and saw the revolver lined on his back. "You pull that trigger and you'll warn the Cherokees that you're back here," he said. "They're not so far ahead that they won't hear the shot."

Sprague spurred ahead, bringing his horse up beside the dun. "Reckon you're right," he said. He started to lower the gun.

Fury saw the flicker in the man's eyes and tried to dodge as Sprague suddenly brought the Colt up and around. He was a fraction of a second too late. The barrel of the gun slammed into the side of his head and knocked him off the bare back of the dun.

He landed hard and rolled over, but before he could get back to his feet, Sprague was on him again, driving a knee into his back and forcing him down. The Ranger grabbed Fury's wrists, jerked them behind him, and whipped a length of rawhide around them.

"Sorry about this, Fury," grunted Sprague. "But I ain't goin' to let you ruin things now." He stood up once Fury was securely tied, then lifted him to his feet. Fury shook his head, trying to dislodge some of the cobwebs that had formed around his brain after being clouted by Sprague.

The other Rangers had seen the commotion at the base of the hill and started riding toward Fury and Sprague, bringing Laurel, Pate, and Frank with them. Sprague helped the groggy Fury back onto the dun as the others rode up.

"What happened, Cap'n?" asked the sandy-haired lieutenant called Proctor.

"Just makin' sure Fury here don't cause any problems when we hit them Cherokees tonight." Sprague gave Laurel and her brothers a hard look. "I'll have you three tied up, too, if I have to. This is Ranger business."

"But . . . but I don't understand," said Laurel, frowning in confusion just like Pate and Frank. "I thought you were going to rescue Felicia."

"We'll see," said Sprague. "But first there's a debt to be paid, and there's only one way to settle it—in redskin blood!"

CHAPTER
18
....

Fury had a throbbing headache from being hit by Sprague, but it was nothing compared to the sickness and anger in his gut. He leaned back against the trunk of the oak behind him and watched the Ranger captain moving around the camp, getting ready for the attack that would be launched once it was good and dark. Sprague looked almost happy.

The only joy in the man's life, figured Fury, came from killing Indians.

Fury's hands were still tied behind his back. His fingers were numb. He had ridden awkwardly with the rest of the group throughout the long afternoon, until Sprague had called a halt and instructed the men to make another cold camp. Sprague and one of his Rangers had ridden ahead to scout out the Cherokees. With the captain gone, Proctor had helped Fury down from the horse and seen to it that he was relatively comfortable.

"Mighty sorry 'bout the way this worked out," the gangling young man had told Fury. "Reckon we got to do what the cap'n tells us, though."

Fury looked up at Proctor. "You know he doesn't care what happens to the Whitelaw girl, whether she lives or dies."

"He cares," insisted Proctor. "Nobody cares more about folks than the cap'n."

Fury had seen he wasn't going to get anywhere arguing with the Rangers about Sprague. They were all devoted to their leader. So he had sat there and seethed, and his anger grew when Sprague and the other man returned to the camp a little later and reported that the Cherokees had settled down for the night about a half-mile upriver. "From the looks of it," Sprague had said, "they don't know there's anybody else around. They'll have sentries out, but once we take care of them, we'll be able to get close to the main bunch 'fore we hit 'em."

125

Fury hoped it worked out that way, that Sprague's optimism was justified. A quick strike, taking the Indians by surprise and wiping them out before they could mount much resistance, was Felicia's best chance for survival.

But even so, that chance was a slim one.

An idea had been brewing in Fury's mind, and he was mulling it over before he suggested it to Sprague. While Fury was thinking, Laurel Whitelaw came up to him, carrying a cold biscuit, a piece of jerky, and a canteen.

"I brought you some food and water," she said as she knelt in front of Fury. "I know it's not much, but it's the best any of us have. I'll help you."

"Thanks," nodded Fury. He opened his lips and took a bite off the biscuit when Laurel held it up to his mouth.

He watched her as he chewed. She had the same sort of defeated look that her brothers wore as they sat with slumped shoulders on the other side of the clearing Sprague had chosen for their camp. With the condition Pate and Frank were both in, there was nothing they could do to oppose Sprague's plans. They had reluctantly told him they would go along with whatever he wanted to do and just pray that Felicia came through it all right. Laurel was just as helpless. She was uninjured, but she couldn't be expected to slip out of the Ranger camp, make her way to the Cherokees, and get Felicia away from them before all hell broke loose.

Fury was the only one with even a hope of succeeding at that, and he was trussed up like a hog.

"Mr. Sprague is certainly looking forward to tonight," said Laurel, her voice trembling a little as she was unable to conceal her worry.

"He's looking forward to it too much," Fury said quietly. "No man should be that anxious to kill."

"You've killed people, though, Mr. Fury. Quite a few, from what I've heard."

He nodded. "I've killed when I had to. If it wasn't for Felicia, I'd probably go along with what Sprague wants. This is different from that bunch he wiped out down southwest of Waco. These Cherokees have turned renegade. Maybe they had a reason for what they did, but that doesn't make up for the innocent folks they killed."

"But they do have Felicia."

"I know," Fury said.

He finished the meager meal in silence, washing down the biscuit and jerky with water from the canteen that Laurel held to his mouth. When he was done, she got ready to stand up, but then she hesitated and her free hand stole under her shirt.

Her back was to the Rangers, so they couldn't see what she was doing as she brought out a short-bladed knife. "I managed to get hold of this and hid it under my shirt," she whispered. "I'll cut you loose."

Fury shook his head. "It'll take time to saw through that rawhide around my wrists. Leave it with me. Make it look like you're helping me shift around a little."

Laurel gave him a miniscule nod and then reached out to help him adjust his position against the rough bark of the tree. As she did so, she left the knife on the ground right behind him.

She stood up and carried the canteen away without looking back. Fury lowered his head, trying to look as dejected as Laurel and her brothers. At the same time, he managed to get his fingers around the handle of the knife and turned the blade so that it touched the rawhide thong around his wrists.

He still wanted to talk to Sprague, but if that didn't work out, at least this way he might have a chance to do something to help Felicia.

Fury had been working on his bonds for about five minutes when Sprague strode over to stand in front of him. Fury quit sawing on the rawhide so that Sprague wouldn't see the tensing of his muscles as he worked the blade back and forth, a fraction of an inch at a time, across the thong.

"How you doin', Fury?" asked Sprague as he squatted down a few feet away.

"Didn't figure you cared," replied Fury.

"Well, you figured wrong. I hate to see a fightin' man in your predicament—but worse than that, I'd hate to see those murderin' Cherokees get away."

"I don't want them to get away, either," Fury told him. "You've got me wrong, Sprague. All I want is to make sure Felicia Whitelaw doesn't get hurt. And I think I've come up with a way to do just that."

Sprague looked and sounded genuinely interested as he said, "What'd that be?"

"If you'll turn me loose, I'll slip into that Indian camp alone, find Felicia, and get her back out in plenty of time for you to start your attack."

Sprague was shaking his head before Fury even finished speaking. He said, "How in the hell do you figure to do that? You ain't invisible, Fury, and you can't make that gal invisible, neither."

"It'll be dark soon," said Fury. "The shadows are already getting thick. I can move pretty quietly when I have to, Sprague."

"Quiet enough that them savages won't hear you?" The Ranger shook his head again. "That ain't likely."

"Wouldn't be the first time I've slipped in and out of an Indian camp without them knowing it. Kit and I walked right into an Arapaho village one night and took out a partner of ours who'd been captured. The Arapahos were saving him for torture, and I reckon they were plenty surprised and disappointed when they found him gone."

"Carson, eh?" grunted Sprague. "Well, I'm not sayin' you didn't do just what you said, Fury, but that don't have anything to do with this. You can't guarantee you wouldn't be caught, and if you was, that'd tip our hand. We need to take the redskins by surprise."

Fury made one last effort. "Even if they caught me sneaking around, they still wouldn't know you and your men were anywhere nearby. I'd be willing to go in unarmed. There wouldn't be anything to tell the Cherokees there are Rangers around."

Sprague took a deep breath, tugged on his short beard, and seemed to be considering the idea for a moment. Then his face hardened. "Nope. Too risky. I'm not takin' any chances on missin' some of those Injuns. The whole bunch has got to die."

"Even if it means Felicia dies, too?"

"I'll hate to see that happen, but . . . yeah, that, too."

Fury met his gaze squarely. "If it works out that way, Sprague, you might as well kill me, too. Otherwise you and I will settle this later."

"Sorry you feel that way, Fury." Sprague sighed, put his hands on his knees, and pushed himself upright again. He put his hand on the butt of his pistol, and for a second, Fury thought Sprague was going to draw the gun and shoot him right here and now. Then Sprague said simply, "Reckon we'll see what happens." He turned and walked away.

Fury slumped back against the tree. He hadn't really expected Sprague to go along with his suggestion, but it would have certainly simplified matters if the captain had been agreeable.

Now, Fury knew he was going to have to escape from the Ranger camp before he could free Felicia Whitelaw. He started sawing on the strand of rawhide again.

The knife Laurel had filched didn't have a particularly sharp blade, so the rawhide was tough going. His grip was clumsy, too, since his fingers were so numb that he could barely feel the handle of the knife. Occasionally it slipped and nicked Fury's wrists, and he felt them becoming slippery with blood. As the last of the sunlight began to fade away and stars winked into life in the darkening sky overhead, Fury increased the pace of his efforts to free himself. Sprague would probably start his attack on the Indian camp within an hour, so that he could move in on the sentries before the moon rose.

Finally, the strands around his wrists parted. He dropped the knife and sank back against the tree again, using its trunk to hide the way he was wiggling his fingers and shaking his hands, trying to restore the circulation to them. Pain shot through his hands as the blood began to flow freely again.

His hands were loose now, one step closer to being free, but there was still a ways to go. He couldn't just get up and stroll off, not with twenty Texas Rangers nearby. He would need something to distract them.

Laurel Whitelaw was sitting about twenty feet away from him, her head down as she stared at the ground. Pate and Frank were beside her. Fury didn't want to call out to her, so he fastened his gaze on the girl and stared at her until instinct told her that she was being watched. She lifted her head, her eyes meeting his.

Fury shifted his shoulders just enough to let her know his arms were free.

In the gloom, Fury couldn't see Laurel's expression well enough to tell if she was surprised, and he certainly couldn't communicate what he wanted her to do. But Laurel was an intelligent young woman; he hoped she was smart enough to know he would need some sort of distraction if he was going to get out of here.

After a moment, Laurel stood up and walked off. Fury watched her intently. Several of the Rangers were moving around the camp, getting ready to ride. Laurel went over to one of the men

who was checking the cinch on his horse's saddle. She talked to
him for a few moments, quietly and too far away for Fury to hear
what she was saying.

Suddenly, she pressed herself against the Ranger, then let out
a scream, placed her hands against the startled man's chest, and
shoved hard. "Leave me alone!" she cried.

"What the hell!" exclaimed the Ranger.

Several men had already turned to watch the disturbance, but
Laurel wasn't finished yet. In a loud voice, she said, "If my father
knew what you just tried to do, he'd horsewhip you!"

"Laurel!" Pate cried, getting unsteadily to his feet and hobbling toward her. Frank came with him. "What is it?"

Laurel poked the Ranger in the chest with her finger. "This
man tried to . . . to make advances to me!" she accused.

"I never—"

"Well, it's certainly not for lack of trying!"

Sprague pushed his way through the crowd that was gathering
around them. "What the devil's goin' on here?" he demanded.

Laurel swung toward him, still not giving the accused Ranger
much chance to talk. "This man attacked me!" she cried.

"Now, darn it, that's just not true!"

Sprague glowered at the man. "What about it, Jordy?" he asked
heavily.

"I just told you, Cap'n! This lady's crazy. I never touched
her—"

"Ha!" interrupted Laurel. "There's no use denying it. Everybody saw you." Her voice was thick with scorn.

"I never touched her," insisted Jordy. "We were just talkin'
about my horse here, and then she sort of fell against me and
commenced to yellin' and pushin' on me. I swear I don't know
what she's talkin' about, Cap'n."

With narrowed, suspicious eyes, Sprague faced Laurel again.
"How about it, Miss Whitelaw? I've known Jordy for a long
time, an' he ain't much of a liar. Are you stickin' to that story
you just told?"

"I certainly am," Laurel sniffed. "It's the truth."

"Wait a minute," said Pate. "Are you saying that my sister is
lying, Captain? What reason would she have for doing that?"

"Durned if I know," replied Sprague. He looked at the other Rangers gathered around them. "Any of you boys see what
happened?"

There was a general shaking of heads and muttering throughout the group. All the men had been too caught up in getting ready for the raid on the Cherokee camp to have been paying much attention to what was going on around them.

Sprague looked at Jordy again. "Well, I reckon it's the lady's word against yours."

"I swear, Cap'n—"

Sprague cut off his protest with a sharp gesture. "Never mind; it's over and done with. From now on, Jordy, keep your hands to yourself and watch your mouth."

"But Cap'n—"

Turning to look sternly at Laurel, Sprague went on, "And if you're lyin', young lady, I expect you to stop it and behave yourself. We got too many other things to worry about right now 'sides any mischief you can come up with."

"Like my sister?" Laurel asked tartly.

"Like teachin' a lesson to them murderin' redskins," snapped Sprague. "Now everybody settle down. We'll be ridin' in less'n an hour."

The captain turned away in disgust, and the ring of Rangers parted to let him through. Sprague had taken only a few steps when some instinct made him stop and peer toward the tree where Fury had been tied up.

A split second later, Sprague was calling in a low but urgent voice, "Mount up! Mount up! We're ridin' *now!*"

John Fury was gone.

CHAPTER
19

· · · · · · · · · · · · · · · · · · · ·

Fury heard a few faint cries far behind him as he ran through the woods along the Brazos, but he didn't slow down. Sprague had said the Cherokees were camped about half a mile upriver. With the lead he had, Fury thought he could run that far before the Rangers caught up with him.

He'd have to move quickly once he reached the Indian camp, though. As soon as Sprague discovered he was gone—which had already happened from the sound of things back there—the Ranger captain would order his men to the attack. They would still approach quietly, hoping to take the Cherokees by surprise, but Sprague wouldn't waste any time in getting there.

That didn't leave Fury any time for stealth or subtlety. He had to get into the camp, grab Felicia Whitelaw, and get the hell out of there as fast as he could before the shooting started.

Fury was grateful for the shadows as he headed quickly along the river. The gathering darkness would make it easier for him to approach the Cherokee camp. At the same time, he wished the southerly breeze would die down; it was liable to carry his scent to the Indian ponies and make them nervous. The Cherokees would be alert for something like that.

He had to risk it, though. There was no time to circle around and approach the camp from the north.

The knife Laurel had given him to cut his bonds was the only weapon he had. His Dragoon Colt would have cut the odds down considerably, but he hadn't seen the gun since Nash had stolen it from him.

That was one more score to settle with Nash if the man was still alive.

Fury slowed his pace when he judged he had come more than a quarter of a mile. He wanted to reach the Cherokee camp before Sprague's Rangers, but he wouldn't do Felicia Whitelaw much

132

good if he stumbled straight into the midst of the Indians and got himself killed. He had to trade a few minutes in return for silence and stealth.

He moved silently through the thick grass along the riverbank, darting from tree to tree. A faint whiff of woodsmoke came to his nose, making him stop in his tracks for a moment. He realized that without him even knowing it, the wind had turned around sometime during the past few minutes. It was blowing out of the north now, carrying the smell of the Cherokees' campfire as well as taking his own scent away from the horses. That was the stroke of sheer luck he needed. Now he had to take advantage of it.

Hurrying before the wind changed again, he spotted the glow of the campfire through the trees. The Cherokees were camped about fifty yards away from the river. Fury angled toward them.

He had taken three more steps when a figure hurtled out from behind a tree and landed on his back.

Fury had a little warning, having picked up a flicker of motion from the corner of his right eye, and he was trying to twist away even as the Cherokee sentry tackled him. He fell heavily, with the Indian on top of him, but the downward thrust of a knife that the Cherokee had aimed at his back missed. The blade embedded itself in the ground instead, although it sliced open the side of Fury's shirt as it passed.

Fury drove an elbow up and back and felt the satisfying jolt as it slammed into the sentry's midsection. So far the Indian hadn't let out a yell, hadn't made a sound, in fact. Fury knew he couldn't count on that continuing until the fight was over.

As the blow from his elbow knocked the Indian aside, Fury writhed over onto his back and lashed out with an open hand. The hard edge of his hand caught the Cherokee in the throat, just as Fury had intended. Gagging, the buckskin-clad brave fell backward. That would keep him from shouting for a few minutes, anyway.

Fury dove after the sentry. His fingers plucked the little knife from behind his belt, and as he landed on the Cherokee, he brought the blade down on the man's chest, putting all of his strength behind the thrust. The Indian stiffened as the point penetrated his body, then he went limp with a rattling sigh that sent foul breath gusting into Fury's face. Fury pushed himself into a sitting position and checked for a pulse.

There wasn't any. The Cherokee was dead.

That was one sentry disposed of, but the fight had taken precious time. Fury lifted his head and listened intently. Were those hoofbeats he heard downriver, or was he just imagining things? Either way, Sprague and the other Rangers were bound to be here soon.

Fury pushed himself to his feet and headed toward the glow of the campfire. When he got closer, he went down to hands and knees and crept forward, using a low screen of brush to conceal himself. Within a couple of minutes, he had reached a point where he could carefully move aside a couple of branches and peer through the opening at the Cherokee camp.

The first thing he had to do was locate Felicia Whitelaw. When the time came for him to move, it would have to be fast and without hesitation.

Some of the Indians were already rolled in their blankets for the night, while others sat near the fire, talking and laughing and gambling. Fury spotted his hat perched on the head of one of them. The Cherokee must have picked it up while they were passing through the deserted camp downriver where Nash and Oakley had finally revealed their treachery.

Fury didn't see Felicia anywhere. And there was no shelter, no lodge where she could be hidden. Fury supposed some of the Cherokees could have taken her off into the trees to rape her, but that was unlikely. They would have enjoyed doing that right in front of their companions, more than likely.

One of the sleeping figures stirred, and Fury caught a flash of blonde hair in the firelight. Relief surged through him. Felicia was all right; she had just retreated into the haven of sleep. Attempted sleep, rather; from the looks of the way she was thrashing around, she was really restless.

Considering everything she had gone through, a few nightmares were more than understandable.

The Indians were looking at Felicia and laughing at her discomfort. Fury felt his anger growing, and with it a sense of helplessness. It probably would have been better if a few of them had her in the woods; he could deal with that more easily than he could with her lying there in plain sight in the glow of the campfire. There was no way he could spirit her away without the Cherokees spotting him.

If he'd had more time, he could have waited until the Indians were all asleep and then tried to reach Felicia. That option had been taken away from him, too. Ben Sprague would see to it that he didn't have any time at all.

In the next instant, gunshots smashed the night.

Fury's head jerked toward the sound, which came from his left, closer to the river. The first shot was the heavy boom of a rifle, followed by a volley of revolver fire. One of the Cherokee sentries must have run into Sprague and the Rangers and gotten one shot off before being cut down by Colts. Hard on the heels of the gunfire came the pounding of hoofbeats.

The camp was suddenly chaos as the Cherokees tried to meet the attack. The ones who had been sleeping rolled out of their blankets and grabbed for their rifles. The others were already on their feet and holding their weapons.

Felicia sat up, a confused, startled look on her drawn features. Blonde hair that had once been thick and lustrous was now lank and tangled around her face.

One of the Cherokees started to run past Fury's position. The chance for subtlety was gone, so he did the only thing he could. He sprang to his feet, looped his left arm around the Indian's neck to jerk him to a halt, and used his right to plunge the knife into the man's back, feeling the blade slice cleanly between the ribs and into the heart.

As the Cherokee stiffened and let out a death cry, Fury reached around him and caught the old single-shot rifle as the Indian started to drop it. The hammer was already pulled back. Fury pointed it one-handed at a nearby Indian and pulled the trigger. The heavy recoil tore the weapon out of his hand, but the rifle had already done its job. The ball slammed into the chest of the second Cherokee and knocked him backward to sprawl lifeless on the ground near Felicia.

Fury yanked his knife out of the first man's back and shoved the corpse aside. "Felicia!" he called. "Over here!"

He probably looked about as frightening to the girl as any of the Cherokees—ragged, blood-spattered, his features haggard from strain. But he was white, and the shouted words in English must have penetrated her stunned brain. She tossed her blankets aside, came to her feet, and started to run toward him.

One of the Cherokees lunged at her, grabbed her shoulder, jerked her back toward him. Fury ran toward them. The Indian thrust the barrel of a rifle past Felicia, using her as a shield as he fired at Fury. Fury threw himself to the side as the muzzle of the rifle belched noise and flame. The ball missed him and screamed off into the trees. Stumbling a little, Fury collided with Felicia and the Cherokee. He reached past the girl and drove the blade into the Indian's throat. A hot torrent of blood flooded over his hand and onto Felicia's back. She screamed.

The Indian collapsed as Fury ripped the knife free of his throat. Fury's other hand closed over Felicia's arm. He didn't intend to be parted from her now. "Come on!" he shouted as he turned to run.

She staggered along beside him as he headed for the trees. The night air was filled with sound now—hoofbeats, gunshots, cries of pain, curses, shouted commands. The Texas Rangers charged through the Indian camp on horseback, shooting madly, right and left. Fury hustled Felicia toward the woods, knowing they'd be just as dead if Ranger lead found them as if the Cherokees had killed them.

Abruptly, a figure loomed up in front of him, a nightmarish shape in the garish, flickering light of the flames. It was one of the braves, holding an empty rifle reversed in his hands so that he could use it as a club. Fury saw the rifle whipping toward him and Felicia, and he shoved the girl out of the way at the last instant. The stock of the rifle crashed into his left shoulder instead, knocking him to one knee and making his left arm go numb. The stock cracked but remained intact, and the Indian wielding the rifle brought it around for another blow.

Fury ducked under it and threw himself forward, tackling the Indian around the knees and bringing him down. The rifle clattered to the ground. Fury had managed to hold onto his knife. He flung himself on the Indian and started to bring the blade down, but the man caught his wrist in a grip of iron before the blade could fall. Using all of his wiry strength, the Cherokee flipped Fury over. Fury wound up with his back on the ground, the Cherokee looming over him and grinning savagely as he fumbled for the tomahawk thrust through a loop on the buckskin pants at his waist.

Unable to wrench his knife hand free, Fury willed his left arm to work as the Indian freed the tomahawk and lifted it for a killing blow. The muscles in Fury's left arm refused to respond. He would be unable to block the tomahawk when it fell to dash his brains out.

Suddenly there was a flicker of movement above and behind

the Cherokee. Felicia had picked up the fallen rifle, and now she swung it with all her strength at the Indian's head. The breech caught him in the back of the skull with a sound like a watermelon breaking. The man grunted and jerked forward. Blood gouted from his nose and his eyes went glassy. The tomahawk slipped from his fingers and fell to the ground beside Fury's head.

Fury shoved the dead man off of him and scrambled to his feet. Felicia stood there, her arms hanging loosely, dropping the shattered rifle as she stared at the back of the Indian's misshapen head. The blow had caved in the man's skull and killed him almost instantly, saving Fury's life.

Feeling was beginning to flow back into Fury's left arm, and with it came pain. He ignored that and grabbed Felicia's hand, pulling her with him as he stumbled toward the trees again. This time they reached the relative safety of the woods, and after they had crashed through the underbrush for several yards, Fury came to a halt.

"Get down and stay down," he told Felicia, pressing on her shoulder until she sank to her knees and crouched behind some bushes. Fury knelt beside her. The shadows were thick here under the trees, and it was unlikely anybody would spot them. Besides, the Indians and the Rangers all had their hands full at the moment.

The battle was still going on, guns crashing and men screaming. This bunch of Cherokees were putting up a much tougher fight than the members of that hunting party who had been killed by Sprague's men. As Fury watched, he saw a couple of the Rangers tumble from their saddles, brought down by rifle fire from the Cherokees.

"Who . . . who are you?" asked Felicia from beside him.

"A friend," Fury told her. "I came out here with your sister and your brothers to get you back."

"My . . . sister? You mean Laurel?" Felicia's voice was hoarse and quavery, showing the strain she had been under.

"Yes. Pate and Frank came, too."

"But where are they?"

"Don't worry about them," Fury assured her. "They're safe. Those are Texas Rangers attacking the camp."

Felicia collapsed against him, shuddering, and Fury slipped an arm around her shoulders to support her. She buried her face against his chest, and sobs wracked her body. Strangled sounds came from her, and after a moment Fury realized she was saying words.

"Safe . . . going to be safe . . . won't hurt me anymore . . ."

He took a deep breath and tried to control the anger raging inside him. Nash's great scheme had backfired this time, and Felicia had wound up in the hands of real Indians, suffering God knows what at their hands. If Nash and Oakley *were* still alive, hanging would be too good for them.

The gunfire was beginning to fade somewhat in the distance. Some of the Cherokees must have managed to make it to their horses, mused Fury, and now the battle had turned into a running fight as the Indians tried to escape.

Sprague wouldn't let them go; Fury was certain of that. The captain would hang on like a bulldog with its teeth sunk in its victim, not letting up until all the Cherokees were dead—even if it cost the lives of his men.

From where they were, Fury couldn't see the clearing where the Indian camp was located very well, so as the gunfire receded even more, he said in a low voice to Felicia, "You stay here while I take a look around."

She clutched desperately at his arm. "No! I . . . I want to go with you."

He could understand why she didn't want to be left alone. After everything she had gone through, he represented at least some measure of security to her. He'd feel a whole hell of a lot better about being able to protect her, though, if he had his hands on a six-gun again.

"All right, come on," he said gently, taking her arm and standing up. "Be careful, though. I think the fighting's over around here, but some of those redskins could still be alive."

Felicia shuddered again, but she didn't falter as she walked with him toward the campsite. Fury took it slow and easy as they approached, his eyes scanning the scene of carnage spread out before them. The hellish light of the flames was pretty appropriate for what they saw.

Bodies were scattered everywhere. Most of them were Cherokees, but there were half a dozen or more dead Rangers sprawled on the ground, too. Fury recognized one of them as the sandy-haired lieutenant called Proctor; he was on his back, staring sightlessly at the night sky, a pair of bullet wounds in his chest.

Fury paused at the edge of the trees. "I've got to get some guns," he told Felicia. "You can stay here. You don't have to go out there."

She swallowed. "I'll go."

Fury grunted, then held her hand tightly as they started across the clearing. He stopped beside Proctor and bent over to pick up the Colt that had fallen from the man's lifeless hand. A quick check of the barrel told Fury it wasn't plugged with dirt. The cylinder had three rounds left in it. He tucked the gun behind his belt, then stooped and picked up another one that had been dropped by one of the other fallen Rangers. This one had two shots left in it.

Fury felt better as he straightened. Five rounds was a lot better than nothing. He could have loaded both guns fully from the dead men's remaining ammunition if he had wanted to take the time, but he was more interested in getting away from here now. As far as he could tell, all of the Indians lying around the camp were dead, but there was no point in taking chances. He wanted to get Felicia back safely to her sister and her brothers.

"Come on," said Fury, taking Felicia's hand again. "Let's get the hell out of here."

"You . . . you're going to take me home?"

Fury looked at her, meeting her stunned eyes and managing a grim smile. "Yes," he said. "I'll take you home."

CHAPTER
20
....

Fury paused for a second more before they left the Indian camp, just long enough to pick up his hat and brush the dirt off it. The Cherokee who had looted it was lying nearby, gutshot. Luckily, none of his blood had gotten on the hat when the Rangers gunned him down.

After settling the hat on his head, Fury took Felicia's arm again and led her away.

They headed downriver, toward the spot where he had left Laurel, Pate, and Frank. Every so often, the sound of a distant shot would drift to their ears, and Fury knew that Sprague and the other Rangers were running the last of the Cherokees to ground.

When he was escaping from the Ranger camp and making his way upriver, Fury had been too busy to pay much attention to landmarks, and now that full night had fallen, he couldn't see much anyway. Still, when half an hour had passed since he and Felicia left the Cherokee camp, he thought they should have reached the others by now. From what he could see by starlight, the landscape was beginning to look a little familiar.

"Hold on a minute," he said quietly to Felicia.

He listened intently but heard nothing, not even the rustle of small animals in the brush. What had happened to the other Whitelaw youngsters? Could they have wandered off after Sprague led his men in the attack on the Indians?

"What is it?" asked Felicia. "What's wrong?"

"Don't know," grunted Fury. "I thought we'd run into your sister and brothers before now."

Felicia shuddered. "Do you think something has happened to them?"

"Shouldn't have. I imagine Sprague left them here by themselves when he went to raid the Cherokee camp."

"Captain Sprague from Fort Fisher?"

Fury nodded. "That's right." They had been walking in silence, but now Fury took advantage of the opportunity to fill Felicia in on some of what had happened, not only to her but also during the days that had followed her kidnapping. She looked more and more aghast as he spoke.

"I . . . I knew something was strange when I realized I was being held prisoner in a root cellar," she said. She drew a deep breath into her body and went on, "When the Cherokees smashed open the door and dragged me out, I saw we were on what looked like a ranch. I didn't understand it, but I never . . . never dreamed white men would do such a thing."

"Reckon Nash and Oakley are about as low as they come," agreed Fury.

"And you don't know what happened to them?"

Fury shook his head.

A shudder ran through Felicia again. "Then they could still be alive out there somewhere?"

"Could be," Fury told her grimly.

"Let's find Laurel and Pate and Frank and get out of here," Felicia said. "I want to go home where I'll be safe."

Fury didn't make any reply, but he knew she might never feel safe again, no matter where she was, not after all she had gone through.

He took her hand. "Come on. We'll look some more."

They trudged along beside the river, Fury keeping his eyes and ears open for any sign of the other Whitelaws. He was beginning to have a very bad feeling about this situation.

A few minutes later, they reached a clearing that Fury definitely recognized. This was where the Rangers had made their cold camp, the place where he had been tied up and leaned against the tree trunk out of the way. Laurel, Pate, and Frank should have still been here unless they had wandered off, and Fury didn't think that was very likely.

"Where the devil . . . ?" muttered Fury as he came to a stop and peered around the clearing. He wished the moon would rise so that he could see better.

"They're lost, aren't they?" asked Felicia, her voice shaking. "Something's happened to them." Fury sensed that she was right on the edge of hysteria again.

"They should've been here." Fury wrapped his fingers around the butt of one of the guns tucked in his belt. He slid out the weapon. "You stay here by the river. I'll take a look around."

"No!—I mean, I'll stay with you."

His jaw tightening, Fury nodded. "All right."

He held the pistol ready, his thumb looped around the hammer, as he moved away from the riverbank and started across the clearing. "Pate!" he called softly. "You here, Pate? Frank? Laurel?"

There was a muffled sound from the underbrush at the far edge of the clearing. Fury stopped in his tracks, and as he did so, Felicia's hand tightened on his left arm. She had heard it, too.

Had the noise been the cry of an animal—or something else? Suddenly, every instinct in Fury's body was shouting an alarm. He shoved Felicia behind him and started to lift the gun, earing back the hammer as he brought the barrel up.

Something crashed out of the brush and leaped toward Fury. He managed to get one shot off before the shadowy figure crashed into him, but the ball went wild, racketing off into the woods. A fist smashed into the side of Fury's head with sickening force, and an instant later arms looped around him, pinning his own arms to his sides as they closed in a brutal grip. He was torn away from Felicia, who shrank back with her hands over her mouth. They failed to stifle the scream that ripped from her throat.

Fury tripped on something and went down. He had been trying to get enough play in his right arm to bring the gun to bear on his attacker, but now his wrist slammed into the ground, and the Colt slipped away from him. His desperately grabbing fingers touched the walnut butt for an instant, but then it was gone. Pain rippled through his body as his assailant rolled over and brought his weight down on Fury's injured left shoulder.

Fury used that pain and his own anger to give himself strength. He brought a knee up and drove it into his attacker's groin, and when the man flinched from that, Fury was able to jerk his right arm free and bring the heel of his hand up sharply into the man's chin. The blow forced back the head of Fury's burly opponent, and the last of the man's grip came loose. Fury rolled to the side, and as he moved away, he lashed out behind him with a booted foot that cracked against the man's jaw.

As he came to his feet, Fury reached for the second gun and looked around quickly for more threats, but he was in no position to meet the one that appeared. A second man stepped out of the woods, and as he lined a six-gun on Fury, he grated in a familiar voice, "Get your hand away from that pistol. Don't move or I'll kill you, you son of a bitch!"

"Nash!"

The name came out of Fury's mouth like the most obscene of curses. The tall, lean Bob Nash just laughed.

"That's right, Fury. I figured it must be you when I saw you had the girl with you. You're damn near the stubbornest bastard I ever met."

A few feet away, Lester Oakley was pushing himself to his feet. He shook his head, flexed his hands, and rolled his brawny shoulders as he got ready to charge at Fury again.

"Hold on, Lester," Nash said sharply. "No need for any more fightin'. Fury's not goin' to cause us any trouble, are you, Fury?"

Fury ignored the question and asked one of his own. "Where are the others?"

"You mean the other three Whitelaw brats?" Nash inclined his head toward the brush. "Wrapped up nice and snug back there. They ain't goin' nowhere—and neither are you."

Fury took a deep breath and tried to calm his racing pulse. Once more, he had to keep his wits about him and try to keep Nash talking. Surely it wouldn't be long until the Rangers came riding back this way; Fury hadn't heard any shots in the distance for quite a while.

"I thought the Cherokees got you and Oakley when they jumped us," he said to Nash. "Was hoping, anyway."

Nash shook his head. The barrel of the gun in his hand didn't waver in the starlight. "Nope. Lester and me got away. Reckon we were mighty lucky. We had our guns, and we found our saddle horses not long after we all scattered. Thing about luck, though, is a man's got to know how to take advantage of it."

"So the two of you decided to hang around and wait for a chance to recoup your losses," guessed Fury.

"That's right. We saw that the Indians had the girl there—" Nash nodded toward Felicia. "—and we figured we might be able to get her back."

"Didn't you wonder how she wound up in their hands?"

"Reckon I know." Nash's voice hardened as he continued, "They must've raided our spread and taken her from there."

"That's right. They killed your wife while they were doing it, along with some of your men."

"Well, I'm sorry about that . . ." Nash hesitated, then added, "But she was only a Comanche, after all. I can find another squaw if I want one. Hell, with the money Lester and I are goin' to have, I can get all the white women I want."

"What money?" asked Fury. "I don't see how you're going to make anything out of this, Nash. You and Oakley would be better off to let us go and head out of here as fast as your horses can carry you. You ever show up around Waco again, there won't be anything waiting for you but a rope."

Oakley laughed harshly. "Hell of a lot you know," he told Fury. "Bob's got it all figured out."

The moon had risen above the trees and was now beginning to cast a silvery light over the clearing. Fury looked at Nash and saw the man was grinning. "Just what have you got figured out?" asked Fury.

"We may have lost that horse herd, but the gal's daddy promised us two thousand dollars if we brought her back. I intend to collect that money."

"What about the rest of us?"

Nash shrugged. "The deal didn't say anything about that. Whitelaw's an honorable man. If Lester and I bring Felicia back, he'll pay us—even if the Indians did kill the rest of you."

"You're insane!" cried Felicia. "You can't tell a lie like that and get away with it. I'll tell my father the truth!"

Nash and Oakley both laughed. It was an ugly sound. "Time we get you back to Waco, little lady, you won't say a damn thing to anybody about what happened. And even if you did, nobody would believe you, not after all you've gone through. They'll just figure you're out of your head after bein' raped and tortured by those redskins and seein' your sister and brothers killed."

Fury felt those cold fingers along his spine again. It was a bold plan Nash had come up with, even more daring than his original one. Harder to put across, too, but he and Oakley would have at least a chance of carrying it off. If they abused Felicia enough during the journey back to Waco, they could easily drive her mind around the bend into lunacy. Other prisoners who had been recovered from Indian captivity in the past had come back unhinged, babbling all sorts of wild tales that no one paid any attention to. If Nash and Oakley ran their bluff successfully, Felicia would fall into that same category.

"Why'd you keep the others alive?" asked Fury, still stalling for time. Close beside him, Felicia had started to cry. Her shoulders shook and she made soft sounds that tore at Fury's insides.

"Figured we'd better keep 'em around until we got our hands on Felicia, just in case we needed some sort of leverage," replied Nash. "Besides, Lester wants to take a few turns with that little Laurel girl before we kill her, and I wouldn't mind samplin' her myself. Man needs a little variety now and then."

The palm of Fury's hand itched to close itself around the butt of the revolver still in his belt. More than anything else at this moment, he wanted to send a bullet smashing into that leering grin of Nash's. But Nash had the drop on him, and even though Fury was fast enough on the draw so that he could probably get a shot off, maybe even kill Nash, Nash would undoubtedly kill him, too.

That would leave Felicia, Laurel, Pate, and Frank to the mercy of Lester Oakley. And mercy was hardly what the brutish man had in mind for them.

"We'd better get movin', Bob," Oakley said anxiously. "If any of them Rangers live through that Injun fight, they're liable to come back this way. I don't want to tangle with *them*."

"You're right, Lester," agreed Nash. "You go tend to Pate and Frank. I'll take care of Fury." The barrel of his gun came up a little more as he lined the sights on Fury's head.

Shooting by moonlight was chancy, Fury thought. He'd have to take a chance on throwing himself aside and grabbing for the gun behind his belt.

The crash of a gunshot came not from Nash's gun but from the direction of the river. Nash jerked back as a slug whined past his ear. Fury spent a fraction of a second glancing toward the Brazos and saw a figure emerging from behind the slight drop of the riverbank. The gun in the man's hand boomed again.

Fury grabbed Felicia's arm and slung her to the ground. She might still be in the line of fire, but at least she would present a smaller target. At the same instant, Nash fired, and Fury felt the heat of the bullet as it passed beside his forearm and ripped the sleeve of his shirt. He went down, rolled, came up palming out the other gun.

The Colt in Fury's hand blasted, recoil shivering up his arm as the weapon bucked heavily against his palm. Through the haze of powdersmoke, in the uncertain moonlight, he saw Nash stagger back a couple of steps.

Oakley had jerked out his own gun, and now he triggered a couple of shots at the figure who had emerged from hiding under the riverbank. The man stumbled and lost his footing, but even as he went down he let loose another shot. From his position on the ground he fired twice more.

One last shot came from Oakley's gun, but it went harmlessly high into the sky as the slugs from the stranger's gun punched into his chest and knocked him backward. He screamed once, a high, thin sound, before he went down and stayed down, his gun falling from slack fingers.

Fury was on one knee watching Nash, who swayed back and forth as he tried to stay on his feet. The barrel of his gun wavered crazily. No point in taking a chance, thought Fury, not when he still had at least one shot left in his own gun.

He aimed carefully and fired, the final shot echoing hollowly in the night air.

Nash's head jerked back as the heavy lead ball smashed into his forehead, bored through his brain, and blew out the back of his skull in a grisly spray of blood, gray matter, and bone splinters. For a couple of seconds, Nash stayed on his feet, already dead even though his body didn't know it yet. Then he folded up in a heap and didn't move again.

Fury didn't spare another glance for Nash. Quickly, he checked the gun in his hand. It was the one that had held three shots when he picked it up, which meant one chamber was still loaded. He strode over to Oakley's body, the pistol trained on the dark hulk, and kicked away the gun Oakley had dropped. A nudge with his booted foot told him Oakley was just as dead as Nash.

They'd never kidnap another girl and trick ransom money out of her terrified parents. The frontier was still a dangerous place to live—for settlers and Indians alike—but one threat had been ended forever.

Fury hurried over to Felicia and lifted her to her feet. She was sobbing and gasping, her emotions driven into a frenzy by the outbreak of violence. Fury tightened his grip on her arm until she looked at him.

"Listen to me," he said sternly. "Your sister and brothers are over there somewhere in the brush. You find them and see if you can untie them, all right? I'm counting on you, Felicia."

She swallowed, gasped a couple more times, then managed to nod. Fury let go of her, and she stumbled toward the brush. He didn't know if she would find Laurel and Pate and Frank or not, but at least looking for them would keep her busy for a few minutes.

That done, Fury went over to the last man, the man who had saved them by showing up when he did. The man was lying on his stomach, his black hat beside him where it had fallen when he pitched forward.

"Turn me over, damn it," rasped a familiar voice.

Fury knelt, took hold of the man's shoulders and carefully rolled him onto his back. "I was wondering when you'd show up, Sprague," said Fury. "You almost waited until it was too late."

Captain Ben Sprague looked up at him, deep-set eyes blinking in the moonlight. The front of his shirt was dark with blood. "Had to . . . come up slow and quiet." he said. "Heard a shot from down here . . . while we were back upriver. Figured you might've . . . run into more trouble."

"So you left the rest of the Rangers upstream and slipped along the riverbank until you could see and hear what was going on?"

"Yeah . . ."

"You kill all those Cherokees?"

"Damn . . . right . . ."

Fury knelt there beside the Ranger, his features set in bleak lines. He knew from the way Sprague sounded, the sucking, bubbling noise when Sprague took a breath, that the captain didn't have much time left. Fury said quietly, "Sprague, you're just about the most ruthless, cold-blooded bastard I've ever met, but for what you did just now . . . thanks."

Sprague's lips moved in either a grimace or a smile, Fury couldn't tell which. "Leastways I'll die . . . lookin' at . . . Texas stars . . . Oh, Lord."

The last was a faint whisper, a mere puff of breath, and Sprague was gone.

Fury stayed where he was for a long moment, until Felicia called from the woods, "Mr. Fury! I found them! But they're tied up and gagged, and I can't get them loose."

Fury looked at Sprague one more time, then stood up and went to help Felicia.

CHAPTER
21
....

Eight of the Rangers had been left alive after the running fight with the Cherokees, not counting Sprague. They came riding up a couple of minutes later, anxious to find out what happened after Sprague had left them behind. They had heard the shooting and knew that something else was wrong.

Fury explained about the gunfight with Nash and Oakley. Felicia had calmed down enough to back up his story, and the surviving Rangers, suspicious at first because they knew of the friction between Fury and Sprague, accepted the truth of the matter. Besides, the bodies of Nash and Oakley were lying in plain sight, and it was hard to argue with their mute, grisly testimony.

The Rangers camped there, and first thing the next morning, Captain Ben Sprague was laid to rest in a grave near the Brazos.

Nash and Oakley were left for the coyotes and the other scavengers, and Fury didn't feel like arguing when the Rangers reached that decision. He was more interested in getting back to Waco.

Laurel, Pate, and Frank were none the worse for their encounter with Nash and Oakley, although the two young men were still weak from their wounds. But they were able to ride, and the whole group started downriver that morning, glad to leave that part of the country behind them. With the winding river and the wooded, rolling hills, the place should have been pretty, but at least for now, it looked to Fury like nothing more than a killing ground.

The good weather held; this time winter was really over, and spring was taking a good strong hold on the land. By late afternoon of the fourth day, the group was nearing the Whitelaw ranch. They had forded the river earlier in the day and were riding along the well-marked trail that followed the southwest bank of the Brazos.

One of the Whitelaw ranch hands was the first to spot them. When he saw the long blonde hair sported by two of the riders, he let out a whoop and slammed his horse into a gallop toward the house. Felicia and Laurel smiled. "He'll let the folks know we're coming," said Laurel. "There ought to be quite a reception waiting for us."

"Yeah," said Frank, still pale but growing stronger as time passed. "If I know Pa, he'll throw a party and invite everybody in McLennan County." He turned to Fury, who was riding beside him on the dun. "You'll come, won't you, Mr. Fury?"

"We'll see," answered Fury noncommittally.

To tell the truth, thought Fury, he was damned tired of this part of Texas, and the sooner he put it behind him, the better as far as he was concerned.

Preston and Muriel Whitelaw were on the front porch of the big whitewashed house when the riders reined up in front of it a few minutes later. Jase Sutton was with them, and it was a toss-up who was grinning the biggest. Tears ran down Muriel's face as she gazed half in disbelief at her sons and daughters, and the eyes of Whitelaw and Sutton were moist, too. Muriel rushed down from the porch as her children dismounted and started hugging them as hard and as fast as she could.

Whitelaw stayed where he was, leaning on his cane and letting his wife have this moment. His eyes met Fury's, and he said simply, "Thank you, sir. I can never thank you enough." Whitelaw looked past Fury and frowned. "Where are Nash and Oakley? What are those Rangers doing with you?"

"That's a long story, Mr. Whitelaw," replied Fury. "I reckon your youngsters can tell you all about it. All I'll say is that Nash and Oakley are dead, and good riddance."

Whitelaw looked more confused than ever, and so did Sutton. The foreman shook his head, then came down from the porch and said, "Light and set for a while. I'll take care of your horse." He looked at the Rangers. "You boys are welcome, too. We'll dig us a cookin' pit over by the bunkhouse and start smokin' a steer. Got some good white lightnin' to wash it down with, too."

The Rangers dismounted and led their horses as Sutton took them to the bunkhouse, where they were greeted boisterously by the ranch hands. Muriel, Felicia, Pate, Frank, and Laurel all went into the house, talking and laughing and crying for joy at being reunited.

That left Fury sitting on his horse and Preston Whitelaw standing on the porch, watching him intently.

"Aren't you coming in, too, Mr. Fury?" asked the rancher.

Fury shook his head. "I never was much of one for family celebrations, Mr. Whitelaw. I'd rather not intrude."

"Intrude?" echoed Whitelaw in surprise. "It's hardly an intrusion. I have a feeling none of my children would be here now if it wasn't for you."

"I thank you kindly, but I'll still be riding."

"Where?"

Fury shrugged. "Back to Waco first, then somewhere on down the trail. San Antonio, probably."

Whitelaw blinked, baffled. "But . . . I owe you. Money, certainly, but more than that—"

"Money'll do just fine. Send a draft for two thousand dollars to the First Bank of San Antonio."

"Of course, if that's what you want. It's worth any amount to me to have my children back safely. But I don't understand."

Neither did Fury, not really. All he knew was that he'd seen enough killing over the last few weeks to last him for a long time. A part of him would have liked to swing down from his saddle and go inside to join the Whitelaws's celebration. But he wasn't really meant for that world; he needed a smoky barroom, a bottle of whiskey, maybe a game of poker, or a woman who'd long since stopped worrying about her virtue. After that, there was always the trail.

Fury smiled at Preston Whitelaw and said, "Those are good kids you've got, every one of them." He lifted a finger to the brim of his hat and sketched a casual salute. "Be seein' you." He turned the dun and heeled it into a trot.

For a long moment, Whitelaw stood there on the porch. Then he turned and went inside to join his family, and John Fury rode away.

SPECIAL PREVIEW!

Giles Tippette, America's new star of the classic
western, tells the epic story of Justa Williams
and his family's struggle for survival . . .

GUNPOINT

By the acclaimed author of
Sixkiller, *Hard Rock*, and *Jailbreak*.

*Here is a special excerpt from this riveting new
novel—available from Jove books . . .*

I was standing in front of my house, yawning, when the messenger from the telegraph office rode up. It was a fine, early summer day and I knew the boy, Joshua, from a thousand other telegrams he'd delivered from Blessing, the nearest town to our ranch some seven miles away.

Only this time he didn't hand me a telegram but a handwritten note on cheap foolscap paper. I opened it. It said, in block letters:

I WILL KILL YOU ON SIGHT JUSTA WILLIAMS

Joshua was about to ride away on his mule. I stopped him. I said, "Who gave you this?" gesturing with the note.

He said, "Jus' a white gennelman's thar in town. Give me a dollar to brang it out to you."

"What did he look like?"

He kind of rolled his eyes. "I never taken no notice, Mistuh Justa. I jest done what the dollar tol' me to do."

"Was he old, was he young? Was he tall? Fat?"

"Suh, I never taken no notice. I's down at the train depot an' he come up an ast me could I git a message to you. I said, 'Shorely.' An' then he give me the dollar 'n I got on my mule an' lit out. Did I do wrong?"

"No," I said slowly. I gave his mule a slap on the rump. "You get on back to town and don't say nothing about this. You understand? Not to anybody."

"Yes, suh," he said. And then he was gone, loping away on the good saddle mule he had.

I walked slowly back into my house, looking at the message and thinking. The house was empty. My bride, Nora, and our eight-month-old son had gone to Houston with the balance of her family for a reunion. I couldn't go because I was Justa Williams and I was the boss of the Half-Moon ranch, a spread of some thirty thousand deeded acres and some two hundred thousand other acres of government grazing land. I was going on for thirty years old and I'd been running the ranch since I was about eighteen when my father, Howard, had gone down through the death of my mother and a bullet through the lungs. I had two brothers, Ben, who was as wild as a March hare, and Norris, the middle brother, who'd read too many books.

For myself I was tired as hell and needed, badly, to get away from it all, even if it was just to go on a two-week drunk. We were a big organization. What with the ranch and other property and investments our outfit was worth something like two million dollars. And as near as I could figure, I'd been carrying all that load for all those years without much of a break of any kind except for a week's honeymoon with Nora. In short I was tired and I was given out and I was wishing for a relief from all the damn responsibility. If it hadn't been work, it had been a fight or trouble of some kind. Back East, in that year of 1899, the world was starting to get sort of civilized. But along the coastal bend of Texas, in Matagorda County, a man could still get messages from some nameless person threatening to kill him on sight.

I went on into the house and sat down. It was cool in there, a relief from the July heat. It was a long, low, Mexican ranch-style house with red tile on the roof, a fairly big house with thick walls that Nora had mostly designed. The house I'd grown up in, the big house, the house we called ranch headquarters, was about a half a mile away. Both of my brothers still lived there with our dad and a few cooks and maids of all work. But I was tired of work, tired of all of it, tired of listening to folks whining and complaining and expecting me to make it all right. Whatever it was.

And now this message had come. Well, it wasn't any surprise. I'd been threatened before so they weren't getting a man who'd come late in life to being a cherry. I was so damned tired that for a while I just sat there with the message in my hand without much curiosity as to who had sent it.

Lord, the place was quiet. Without Nora's presence and that of my eight-month-old heir, who was generally screaming his head off, the place seemed like it had gone vacant.

For a long time I just sat there, staring at the brief message. I had enemies aplenty but, for the life of me, I couldn't think of any who would send me such a note. Most of them would have come busting through the front door with a shotgun or a pair of revolvers. No, it had to be the work of a gun hired by someone who'd thought I'd done him dirt. And he had to be someone who figured to cause me a good deal of worry in addition to whatever else he had planned for me. It was noontime, but I didn't feel much like eating even though Nora had left Juanita, our cook and maid and maybe the fattest cook and maid in the county, to look after me. She came in and asked me in Spanish what I wanted to eat. I told her nothing and, since she looked so disappointed, I told her she could peel me an apple and fetch it to me. Then I got up and went in my office, where my whiskey was, and poured myself out a good, stiff drink. Most folks would have said it was too hot for hard liquor, but I was not of that mind. Besides, I was mighty glum. Nora hadn't been gone quite a week out of the month's visit she had planned, and already I was mooning around the house and cussing myself for ever giving her permission to go in the first place. That week had given me some idea of how she'd felt when I'd been called away on ranch business of some kind or another and been gone for a considerable time. I'd always thought her complaints had just come from an overwrought female, but I reckoned it had even been lonelier for her. At least now I had my work and was out and about the ranch, while she'd mostly been stuck in the house without a female neighbor nearer than five miles to visit and gossip with.

Of course I could have gone and stayed in the big house; returned to my old ways just as if I were still single. But I was reluctant to do that. For one thing it would have meant eating Buttercup's cooking, which was a chore any sane man would have avoided. But it was considerably more than that; I'd moved out and I had a home and I figured that was the place for me to be. Nora's presence was still there; I could feel it. I could even imagine I could smell the last lingering wisps from her perfume.

Besides that, I figured one or both of my brothers would have some crack to make about not being able to stand my own company or was I homesick for Mommy to come back. We knew each other like we knew our own guns and nothing was off limits as far as the joshing went.

But I did want to confer with them about the threatening note. That was family as well as ranch business. There was nobody, neither of my brothers, even with Dad's advice, who was capable of running the ranch, which was the cornerstone of our business. If something were to happen to me we would be in a pretty pickle. Many years before I'd started an upgrading program in our cattle by bringing in Shorthorn cattle from the Midwest, Herefords, whiteface purebreds, to breed to our all-bone, horse-killing, half-crazy-half-wild herd of Longhorns. It had worked so successfully that we now had a purebred herd of our own of Herefords, some five hundred of them, as well as a herd of some five thousand crossbreds that could be handled and worked without wearing out three horses before the noon meal. Which had been the case when I'd inherited herds of pure Longhorns when Howard had turned the ranch over to me.

But there was an art in that crossbreeding and I was the only one who really understood it. You just didn't throw a purebred Hereford bull in with a bunch of crossbred cows and let him do the deciding. No, you had to keep herd books and watch your bloodlines and breed for a certain conformation that would give you the most beef per pound of cow. As a result, our breeding program had produced cattle that we easily sold to the Northern markets for nearly twice what my stubborn neighbors were getting for their cattle.

I figured to go over to the big house and show the note to my brothers and Howard and see what they thought, but I didn't figure to go until after supper. It had always been our custom, even after my marriage, for all of us to gather in the big room that was about half office and half sitting room and sit around discussing the day's events and having a few after-supper drinks. It was also then when, if anybody had any proposals, they could present them to me for my approval. Norris ran the business end of our affairs, but he couldn't make a deal over a thousand dollars without my say-so. Of course that was generally just a formality since his was the better judgment in such matters. But there had to be just one boss and that was me. As I say, a situation I was finding more and more wearisome.

I thought to go up to the house about seven of the evening. Juanita would have fixed my supper and they would have had theirs, and we'd all be relaxed and I could show them the note and get their opinion. Personally, I thought it was somebody's idea of a prank. If you are going to kill a man it ain't real good policy to warn him in advance.

About seven I set out walking toward the big house. It was just coming dusk and there was a nice breeze blowing in from the gulf. I kept three saddle horses in the little corral behind my house, but I could walk the half mile in just about the same time as it would take me to get up a horse and get him saddled and bridled. Besides, the evening was pleasant and I felt the need to stretch my legs.

I let myself into the house through the back door, passed the door to the dining room, and then turned left into the big office. Dad was sitting in his rocking chair near to the door of the little bedroom he occupied. Norris was working at some papers on his side of the big double desk we shared. Ben was in a straight-backed chair he had tilted back against the wall. The whiskey was on the table next to Ben. When I came in the room he said, "Well, well. If it ain't the deserted bridegroom. Taken to loping your mule yet?"

I made a motion as if to kick the chair out from under him and said, "Shut up, Ben. You'd be the one to know about that."

Howard said, "Any word from Nora yet, son?"

I shook my head. "Naw. I told her to go and enjoy herself and not worry about writing me." I poured myself out a drink and then went and sat in a big easy chair that was against the back wall. Norris looked up from his work and said, "Justa, how much higher are you going to let this cattle market go before you sell off some beef?"

"About a week," I said. "Maybe a little longer."

"Isn't that sort of taking a gamble? The bottom could fall out of this market any day."

"Norris, didn't anybody ever tell you that ranching was a gamble?"

"Yes," he said, "I believe you've mentioned that three or four hundred times. But the point is I could use the cash right now. There's a new issue of U.S. treasury bonds that are paying four percent. Those cattle we should be shipping right now are about to reach the point of diminishing returns."

Ben said, "Whatever in the hell that means."

I said, "I'll think it over." I ragged Norris a good deal and got him angry at every good opportunity, but I generally listened when he was talking about money.

After that Ben and I talked about getting some fresh blood in the horse herd. The hard work was done for the year but some of our mounts were getting on and we'd been crossbreeding within the herd too long. I told Ben I thought he ought to think about getting a few good Morgan studs and breeding them in with some of our younger quarter horse mares. For staying power there was nothing like a Morgan. And if you crossed that with the quick speed of a quarter horse you had something that would stay with you all day under just about any kind of conditions.

After that we talked about this and that, until I finally dragged the note out of my pocket. I said, not wanting to make it seem too important, "Got a little love letter this noon. Wondered what ya'll thought about it." I got out of my chair and walked over and handed it to Ben. He read it and then brought all four legs of his chair to the floor with a thump and read it again. He looked over at me. "What the hell! You figure this to be the genuine article?"

I shrugged and went back to my chair. "I don't know," I said. "I wanted to get ya'll's opinion."

Ben got up and handed the note to Norris. He read it and then raised his eyebrows. "How'd you get this?"

"That messenger boy from the telegraph office, Joshua, brought it out to me. Said some man had given him a dollar to bring it out."

"Did you ask him what the man looked like?"

I said drily, "Yes, Norris, I asked him what the man looked like but he said he didn't know. Said all he saw was the dollar."

Norris said, "Well, if it's somebody's idea of a joke it's a damn poor one." He reached back and handed the letter to Howard.

Dad was a little time in reading the note since Norris had to go and fetch his spectacles out of his bedroom. When he'd got them adjusted he read it over several times and then looked at me. "Son, I don't believe this is something you can laugh off. You and this ranch have made considerable enemies through the years. The kind of enemies who don't care if they were right or wrong and the kind of enemies who carry a grudge forever."

"Then why warn me?"

Norris said, "To get more satisfaction out of it. To scare you."

I looked at Dad. He shook his head. "If they know Justa well enough to want to kill him they'll also know he don't scare. No, there's another reason. They must know Justa ain't all that easy to kill. About like trying to corner a cat in a railroad roundhouse. But if you put a man on his guard and keep him on his guard, it's got to eventually take off some of the edge. Wear him down to where he ain't really himself. The same way you buck down a bronc. Let him do all the work against himself."

I said, "So you take it serious, Howard?"

"Yes, sir," he said. "I damn well do. This ain't no prank."

"What shall I do?"

Norris said, "Maybe we ought to run over in our minds the people you've had trouble with in the past who've lived to bear a grudge."

I said, "That's a lot of folks."

Ben said, "Well, there was that little war we had with that Preston family over control of the island."

Howard said, "Yes, but that was one ranch against another."

Norris said, "Yes, but they well knew that Justa was running matters. As does everyone who knows this ranch. So any grudge directed at the ranch is going to be directed right at Justa."

I said, with just a hint of bitterness, "Was that supposed to go with the job, Howard? You didn't explain that part to me."

Ben said, "What about the man in the buggy? He sounds like a likely suspect for such a turn."

Norris said, "But he was crippled."

Ben gave him a sour look. "He's from the border, Norris. You reckon he couldn't hire some gun help?"

Howard said, "Was that the hombre that tried to drive that herd of cattle with tick fever through our range? Those Mexican cattle that hadn't been quarantined?"

Norris said, "Yes, Dad. And Justa made that little man, whatever his name was, drive up here and pay damages."

Ben said, "And he swore right then and there that *he'd* make Justa pay damages."

I said, "For my money it's got something to do with that maniac up in Bandera County that kept me locked up in a root cellar for nearly a week and then tried to have me hung for a crime I didn't even know about."

"But you killed him. And damn near every gun hand he had."

I said, "Yeah, but there's always that daughter of his. And there was a son."

Ben gave me a slight smile. "I thought ya'll was close. I mean *real* close. You and the daughter."

I said, "What we done didn't have anything to do with anything. And I think she was about as crazy as her father. And Ben, if you ever mention that woman around Nora, I'm liable to send you one of those notes."

Norris said, "But that's been almost three years ago."

I shook my head. "Time ain't nothing to a woman. They got the patience of an Indian. She'd wait this long just figuring it'd take that much time to forget her."

Norris said skeptically, "That note doesn't look made by a woman's hand."

I said, "It's block lettering, Norris. That doesn't tell you a damn thing. Besides, maybe she hired a gun hand who could write."

Ben said, "I never heard of one."

Howard said, waving the note, "Son, what are you going to do about this?"

I shrugged. "Well, Dad, I don't see where there's anything for me to do right now. I can't shoot a message and until somebody either gets in front of me or behind me or *somewheres,* I don't see what I can do except keep a sharp lookout."

The next day I was about two miles from ranch headquarters, riding my three-year-old bay gelding down the little wagon track that led to Blessing, when I heard the whine of a bullet passing just over my head, closely followed by the crack of a distant rifle. I never hesitated; I just fell off my horse to the side away from the sound of the rifle. I landed on all fours in the roadbed, and then crawled as quick as I could toward the sound and into the high grass. My horse had run off a little ways, surprised at my unusual dismount. He turned his head to look at me, wondering, I expected, what the hell was going on.

But I was too busy burrowing into that high grass as slow as I could so as not to cause it to ripple or sway or give away my position in any other way to worry about my horse. I took off my hat on account of its high crown, and then I eased my revolver out of its holster, cocking it as I did. I was carrying a .42/.40 Navy Colt, which is a .40-caliber cartridge chamber on a .42-caliber frame. The .42-caliber frame gave it a good weight in the hand with less barrel deviation, and the .40-caliber bullets it fired would stop anything you hit in the right place. But it still wasn't any match for a rifle at long range, even with the six-inch barrel. My enemy, whoever he was, could just sit there patiently and fire at the slightest movement, and he had to eventually get me because I couldn't lay out there all day. It was only ten of the morning, but already the sun was way up and plenty hot. I could feel a little trickle of sweat running down my nose, but I dasn't move to wipe it away for fear even that slight movement could be seen. And I couldn't chance raising my head enough to see for that too would expose my position. All I could do was lay there, staring down at the earth, and wait, knowing that, at any second, my bushwhacker could be making his way silently in my direction. He'd have to know, given the terrain, the general location of where I was hiding.

Of course he might have thought he'd hit me, especially from the way I'd just fallen off my horse. I took a cautious look to my left. My horse was still about ten yards away, cropping at the grass along the side of the road. Fortunately, the tied reins had fallen behind the saddle horn and were held there. If I wanted to make a run for it I wouldn't have to spend the time gathering up the reins. The bad part of that was that our horses were taught to ground-rein. When you got off, if you dropped the reins they'd stand there just as if they were tied to a stump. But this way my horse was free to wander off as the spirit might move him. Leaving me afoot whilst being stalked by a man with a rifle.

I tried to remember how close the bullet had sounded over my head and whether or not the assassin might have thought he'd hit me. He had to have been firing upward because there was no other concealment except the high grass. Then I got to thinking I hadn't seen a horse. Well, there were enough little depressions in the prairie that he could have hid a horse some ways back and then come forward on foot and concealed himself in the high grass when he saw me coming.

But how could he have known I was coming? Well, that one wasn't too hard to figure out. I usually went to town at least two or three times a week. If the man had been watching me at all he'd of known that. So then all he'd of had to do was come out every morning and just wait. Sooner or later he was bound to see me coming along, either going or returning.

But I kept thinking about that shot. I'd had my horse in a walk, just slouching along. And God knows, I made a big enough target. In that high grass he could easily have concealed himself close enough for an easy shot, especially if he was a gun hand.

The more I thought about it the more I began to think the shooter had been aiming to miss me, to scare me, to wear me down as Howard had said. If the note had come from somebody with an old grudge, they'd *want* me to know who was about to kill me or have me killed. And a bushwhacking rifle shot wasn't all that personal. Maybe the idea was to just keep worrying me until I got to twitching and where I was about a quarter of a second slow. That would be about all the edge a good gun hand would need.

I'd been laying there for what I judged to be a good half hour. Unfortunately I'd crawled in near an ant mound and there was a constant stream of the little insects passing by my hands. Sooner or later one of them was going to sting me. By now I was soaked in sweat and starting to get little cramps from laying so still. I knew I couldn't stay there much longer. At any second my horse might take it into his head to go loping back to the barn. As it was he was steadily eating his way further and further from my position.

I made up my mind I was going to have to do something. I cautiously and slowly raised my head until I could just see over the grass. There wasn't anything to see except grass. There was no man, no movement, not even a head of cattle that the gunman might have secreted himself behind.

I took a deep breath and moved, jamming my hat on my head as I did and ramming my gun into its holster. I ran, keeping as low as I could, to my horse. He gave me a startled look, but he didn't spook. Ben trains our horses to expect nearly anything. If they are of a nervous nature we don't keep them.

I reached his left side, stuck my left boot in the stirrup, and swung my right leg just over the saddle. Then, hanging on to his side, I grabbed his right rein with my right hand and pulled his head around until he was pointing up the road. I was holding on to the saddle with my left hand. I kicked him in the ribs as best I could, and got him into a trot and then into a lope going up the road toward town. I tell you, it was hell hanging on to his side. I'd been going a-horseback since I could walk, but I wasn't no trick rider and the position I was in made my horse run sort of sideways so that his gait was rough and awkward.

But I hung on him like that for what I judged to be a quarter of a mile and out of rifle shot. Only then did I pull myself up into the saddle and settle myself into a normal position to ride a horse. Almost immediately I pulled up and turned in the saddle to look back. Not a thing was stirring, just innocent grass waving slightly in the light breeze that had sprung up.

I shook my head, puzzled. Somebody was up to something, but I was damned if I could tell what. If they were trying to make me uneasy they were doing a good job of it. And the fact that I was married and had a wife and child to care for, and a hell of a lot more reason to live than when I was a single man, was a mighty big influence in my worry. It could be that the person behind the threats was aware of that and was taking advantage of it. If such was the case, it made me think more and more that it was the work of the daughter of the maniac in Bandera that had tried in several ways to end my life. It was the way a woman would think because she would know about such things. I couldn't visualize the man in the buggy understanding that a man with loved ones will cling harder to life for their sake than a man with nothing else to lose except his own hide.

If you enjoyed this book, subscribe now and get...

TWO FREE

A $7.00 VALUE—

A special offer for people who enjoy reading the best Westerns published today.

WESTERNS!

NO OBLIGATION

Mail the coupon below

To start your subscription and receive 2 FREE WESTERNS, fill out the coupon below and mail it today. We'll send your first shipment which includes 2 FREE BOOKS as soon as we receive it.

Mail To: **True Value Home Subscription Services, Inc. P.O. Box 5235**
120 Brighton Road, Clifton, New Jersey 07015-5235

YES! I want to start reviewing the very best Westerns being published today. Send me my first shipment of 6 Westerns for me to preview FREE for 10 days. If I decide to keep them, I'll pay for just 4 of the books at the low subscriber price of $2.75 each; a total $11.00 (a $21.00 value). Then each month I'll receive the 6 newest and best Westerns to preview Free for 10 days. If I'm not satisfied I may return them within 10 days and owe nothing. Otherwise I'll be billed at the special low subscriber rate of $2.75 each; a total of $16.50 (at least a $21.00 value) and save $4.50 off the publishers price. There are never any shipping, handling or other hidden charges. I understand I am under no obligation to purchase any number of books and I can cancel my subscription at any time, no questions asked. In any case the 2 FREE books are mine to keep.

Name _____

Street Address _____ Apt. No. _____

City _____ State _____ Zip Code _____

Telephone _____

Signature _____
(if under 18 parent or guardian must sign)

Terms and prices subject to change. Orders subject
to acceptance by True Value Home Subscription
Services. Inc.

13485-7